Other books by Sherrie DeMorrow:

Knight and Daye
Cloud of Dreams
The Elder Rose
All The Land
The Little Bird
Beyond the Land

BEYOND THE LAND

BY

SHERRIE DEMORROW

Published 2018 by

Lightning Source (UK) Ltd
Chapter House,
Pitfield,
Kiln Farm,
Milton Keynes
MK11 3LW,
UK

Cover Art Design by Sam Wall

To LL for help and support

To the memories of RC, T-T, IC, LO, CH, VM and especially AC,

who continues to inspire my work

PREFACE

Please note **this is a book of fiction** and **NOT** meant as an accurate representation of historical events. The reader must suspend all preconceptions of belief in past history. There may be some reality in detail to it, but most of the scenarios are FAKE.

The historical attitudes towards sensitive issues, and people's prejudices of the time, had to remain intact to provide a sense of realism in the story.

Some place names given are **NOT** real, unless otherwise stated or recognised as real. Other characters (for the most part) are fictional and loosely based on people known of by the author.

CHAPTER I

The island of Clunia lay in the waters, near a coastal town called Pallancium, in the Roman province of Britannia. It was relatively small place, populated by strange beings called Mercastes. A Mercaste was someone of a human/fish combination, the lower half demonstrating the latter. The females were referred to as mermaids, the men, as mermen... *but who needs to be pedantic?* We were a benign group, occasionally fitting in amongst the Mortals (a word we used to describe humanity). Luckily, most Mortals would be accepting, sometimes giving them odd bits of cloth or old tunics to cover up when the Mercastes would swim ashore and into the public eye. Some Mortals would be curious, but if not for that, there would be scathing prejudice... a trait noticeable in the majority of Mortals. Mercastes would do no harm to anyone, nor wish to; yet, the Mortals looked with disdain upon us, with the term *freeloader* hoisted at the top of their mind.

For much of the time, we did swimming rounds, helping distressed Mortals at sea and sunning ourselves on Clunia's sandy shores, resting coolly under the trees or bushes. Mercastes lived in most of the world's oceans, (at least those known of!). Those of the Clunian persuasion, of which I am a part, were the most laid back of them. This was possibly the reason for the Mortal assumption of our freeloading... too relaxed in *their* minds.

It was good to be relaxed in the sun and spread the fins out. A quirk of our species is that if we stay out of the water too long, we gain our land legs, and look like Mortals, at least from a distance. Staying dry was not a huge problem, but if landed for too long, some of us would become ill, usually with a headache and other indications of discomfort. After all, we received Neptune's kiss and converted to the ways of the sea. Mercastes were usually outcasts from society, either by one's choice to escape society, or from falling foul of the legal system. Those who fell foul of the system were given the option to live out their lives *in the sea*, as an alternative to execution or a term of imprisonment.

This time of the year was much hotter than I remembered. Mortals dropped like flies, as the Mercastes took to the ocean. Scorched by the sun's relevant heat, Mortals, dying for cover, ran to the town's buildings... havens nesting within their historical spaces. Temples to the gods took in the more religious folk, who prayed within its sacred shield, blotting out the period of intensity. As the unbearable summer wore on, there was difficulty in getting crops available and famines resulted, forcing many into starvation and death. Those who survived sought food from the waters, casting out nets in desperation for a bite to eat. Inevitably, this action led to conflict between Mercastes and Mortals.

Although there were plenty of fish in the sea, some of them were for *us* to eat. Mortals had a reputation for depleting our food sources and we needed help from our fellow creatures called Sirens. The Sirens came from another area of the world, but were happy to make their way to Clunia and converse with our people to find a ready solution to this. As we loved Mortals and considered them friends, unless otherwise noted, the Sirens had an antipathy toward them... they referred to it as *odium*. Sirens would use their odium against Mortals by singing pleasurable tunes and calling out to them (sometimes by name if they could catch it). The Mortal would instinctively burrow out of his mental hole to enquire what was going on. We did not have to think far with regard to the outcome, as Mortal remains came floating off into the deeper seas, where the larger fish species usually had a hand (or fin) involved.

I spent most of my days swimming, going past craggy, old rock pools; then on one occasion, diving beneath the sea, I found a downed wreck to explore. I went through the lower decks, seeing the former sumptuousness the Mortals liked to call home, when on holiday.

They were paired in delight, these worldly rooms;
Embarking on a journey that ended too soon.

The rest of the self-made poem slipped the mind, seeing that all was fair and the air had matured over time. It was sad, considering the loss of hundreds, I figured. Yet, it was for their twitchy cause, sailing upon our realm, like a kitchen maid on a bunk. There was no personal effects to go through, but for a dislodged jewel that separated from the main hoard. Any one of us could come up and take for ourselves, but as we did not think like Mortals, our personal possessions were sparse. Anything found from these mystical wrecks could be kept and/or shared. The items never found their way into museums, and we at times used them as keepsakes between treasured friends, either man or maid. We were not in competition with Mortals, but we thought our way was slightly better, and more *freer*.

I swam away from the Mortal design to find the open sea, where multitudes of fish lived together. These fish came in all shades, colours, and objectives. Some of the time, they were also corpses, but we did not hold *that* against them. We all swam together, harmoniously with no prejudice, and certainly nothing *personal* came between us. However, when it came to food, things proved slightly more touchy...

I was once a Mortal myself, called Alexander Nespor, until I received Neptune's Kiss. A married man I was, with two beautiful children created from the precious union. We had a good thirteen years together, until the wife had looked another way and began an affair with someone she once knew, before I came into her life. It got to the point when we had many too disagreements together and I found she had brainwashed our children against me... just so she could get what *she* wanted...

...*oooh, it burned me inside to remember the past.*

However, I was too optimistic during those thirteen years. I thought my estate was secured and my family and I were going places.

This, unfortunately, was not to be. As far as I could tell, it was not *me* who rocked boats. True, I spent my married life working in the Amphitheatre; (a combined Grecian term roughly meaning, 'a place for viewing on both sides'... *that is how I saw it, anyway).* The long hours of performing and demands took their toll and, I must confess, the family was neglected somewhat. I still had to earn a living for them and it was for *them* I had worked so hard. I did have admirers, but I never crossed the line, mind you. Neptune's Kiss had freed me from this ungodly relationship, and I let the divorce go through, so the wife could get what she wanted... *from another.*

Pallancium had complex laws and my wife had 'friends', so strings were pulled and favours taken, in order to have her legally emancipated from me, and that she, alone, had the children. I must admit that it was humiliating and I felt accursed that she influenced the legal bodies to eject me from society and into the sea. I bore no grudges against her, though, nor had I attempted to regain my paternal status with my children. It had been a different journey, but I had hoped the family adjusted well without me. I was completely cut off, never to be heard from again... at least as a Mortal...

... and Neptune's Kiss released me from that Mortal world.

As an afterthought, life beyond the land was more instinctual, with underwritten rules of common sense, laden in the minds of all sea life. Pallancium rules, I believe, favoured those who were in *control*. If one was not, then, one would be a damn sight for it. It was a scary notion and I felt it better left to where it belongs, along with my former wife, who I bear nothing but a good riddance to. One lives loosely in the water, swimming around to the heart's content, having a bite to eat and sunning oneself on the Clunian shore. Sunbathing was a happy pastime for us and it was not unsavoury to stay out of the water, but one could not do this for *too* long... the lack of water would get to us.

Thus, I was sent by the stars (or rather inflamed Mortals) to live out my days, *elsewhere*. The Mercastes around me were also once on Mortal ground. We never discussed the stories of our past lives, and decided we keep that to ourselves. Although I was not very young anymore, I was not too old and still thought to be a handsome gentleman. I really enjoyed watching the female folk ashore find their land legs. The sight became somewhat amusing when the stronger males, (who were already landed), had lifted them out of the water, with female fins flipping around in the air. Once they were settled, the girls would lay out and relax, drying off nicely. Some of them were rather pretty, but I was not ready, nor willing, to play the field. I could not understand or fathom how these girls ended up as society's outcasts, like the rest of us. I mostly kept to myself, especially since my bad experiences dictated my immediate actions. I had a few friends, but they were rather superficial and I figured it was every man for himself.

Still, it was for a time we stayed dry, until our bodies screamed for moisture. It was not a pleasant spell when we fell ill, as the naked exodus toward the sea proved a point to many. When some of us did manage to swim as far as Pallancium, we had to play it cool and careful. Though many were discouraged from interacting with us, we did appreciate those who took the care, regarding clothing and well-being.

The inquisitiveness of some of the finest Mortal minds about the oceanic world and the many lives beneath, led them to 'invite' us over to their Aquarium... *to be put on display*. It was an opportunity get the Mortals to view all sea creatures up-close; their interest focusing on Mercastes to make a show for them, by having us swimming alongside full-born fish.

It so happened that it could never be a permanent display. The powers-that-be would have the tanks emptied in the evenings for cleaning, via a huge vacuum.

When fresh water was pumped into the tanks, many sea creatures were scooped from their daily lives and thrown haphazardly together into a watery circus. Overall, we did not mind showing our fins off to the intense Mortal's gaze, but there were times some of the fish had *better* things to do. Families of various species were broken up, just for the sake of getting the single member on view to the Mortal public. When the generator was switched on to gather us illustrious beings, we would all brace ourselves in and endure the storm that awaited us.

So, it was difficult for us not to be set for capture for the day, or week, of exhibitions. It depended on Mortal demand, a ploy to which we were all sucked in.

At times, I would wish that Neptune Himself would put that nonsensical thing out of commission!

One day, that vacuum caught up with me and I, too, was sucked into the Mortal darkness. I did not have a family of sorts down in the sea; so, I went with the flow, as it was a temporary situation. My old family were long gone, so there was none to care for. My current friends were just acquaintances who were the 'pass the salt' types, whereby the conversation never reached its full capacity.

I soon realised I was placed into that circus tank, along with many others. They were not very happy about their newfound situation and it clearly shown on their faces. There were some who were right cross, as they had appointments to keep. *Just because one was a fish did not mean one was idle!*

I swam endlessly around in the tank, taking in my daily exercise, trying not to think about the encapsulation I was facing. I tried not to take it seriously, lest depression set in.

However, I saw a piranha, who was on holiday, complaining to his cohort about being late for his return trip home. Sea horses entertained dozens of little sea bass, who loved to ride his back, forgetting about the predicament they were in.

A tiger fin came up to me with a worried look that spoke volumes.

He said to me, 'My wife and children were having a good swish in the sea, 'til I got separated from them, just a moment ago, with their voices ringing in my ears. I was put among a crowd of serpentines and it was not nice at all. What will become of us?!'

What will become of us, indeed?

'We shan't be here for long, maybe a day or so, if we are lucky. Once the generator is turned on, we can make a break for it and leave. I wouldn't worry. Your family, at least, should be safe, if not here already.'

He looked at me with his beady eye. 'At least *you* have no one to care for!'

And he swam away... leaving me to bide my time in this Circus.

CHAPTER II

The coastal town of Pallancium, Britannia, was conquered by the Romans in the century after the initial conquest of AD 43. The Mercaste island of Clunia lay beyond, separated by a Narrow Strait. Pallancium's multicultural society adapted to Roman ways and means. Some people there claimed foreign birth, but were drawn to Pallancium for the heady mix of the exotic and practical, or to throw away the book and rewrite new lives for themselves. The indigenous people who lived there became subservient to Rome. Fashions changed accordingly, though some kept to their traditional clothing, incorporating Roman designs into the woven cloth. Everyone loved their cloaks and tunics, whilst Greek-style togas never caught on. Usual points of authority were met within Pallancium municipality, tethered to Roman legality and power.

Entertainments were taken very seriously by the Pallancium people. Activities varied from festivals to the gods, chariot racing, and gladiator combats. A favourite of society was one Cheston Ben-Phurr, who relished these feverish dramatics. Other gayeties included theatre, museum perusal, and artistries of all sorts. One of the main features that gave this society never ending fascination was aquarium exhibitions. Varied fish gathered from the seas into a huge vacuum, powered by fantastic generators. Spectators would gasp and gosh at the beauty of the many species that swirled their fins around the tank, with grace and agility. There was a curiosity about sea-life, and the Mercastes were no exception.

Nanlee Q. Pymbrush was Chief Research Scientist at the Aquarium, spending many hours investigating the captured creatures from the deep. He demonstrated ideas of humane treatment, much to the chagrin of his betters; it was mere luck that his idea of daily cleaning of the tank was enacted, which allowed a plethora of different fish to enter the system hygienically. This made for more study, and Pymbrush enjoyed it, spending much of his schedule in doing so.

'They are part of our ecology and good for the environment, for without them, there would be a planetary imbalance,' he would argue to his superiors.

To which they would retort back, 'They are plentiful, edible and it is *you*, sir, who are imbalanced.'

Pymbrush sighed, unable to fight the inevitable; at other times, he would so wish that the current counsel would retire to let new blood in with fresh ideas. He was an ordinary gentleman, mid-thirties, brushed back sand-coloured hair, blue eyes, with a slight look of a chipmunk, which was very endearing. With a warm personality, he would try to be at his best, and try not to let anyone down, be it at work or on a date. Unmarried, and soberly lamenting his sorry state of bachelorhood, he lived alone in a block of flats, usually keeping to himself...

...but he *was* in the process in the wooing of one young maid called Cynthia Tarquinne.

Cynthia did take interest in Pymbrush. She fancied his shine-about warmth, gentlemanly manners, and predictable nature. Most people would find it tiresome, but she stubbornly refused to follow this precedence and carried on dating him. She was the daughter of the fishing industrialist, Laurent Tarquinne, recently deceased from illness. The mother had died since her birth, as Cynthia entered the world through the caesarean exit. Due to lack of female influence, she acquired tomboyish attributes and grew up in the company of her father and his various male cohorts (though it was unproved this was of an intimate nature). Thus, she saw all men as her friends and equals. Women were irrelevant to her, but as she came of age, she felt them to be a threat. However, her relationship with Pymbrush was secure and she knew *no one* would want him.

She was well-treated by her father's friends, since his demise. She saw them as surrogate 'uncles' and became fond of them, especially as they refrained from interfering with her life. Cynthia stood at just under five feet, had brown eyes, long honey-coloured hair with a fringe at the forehead, and reasonably good-looking. It was realistic that she would never win a beauty contest, and she left that to the professionals who knew their own confidence. She was confident, but her version just grasped its talent elsewhere. That did not make *her* a lousy catch; it just made her a different personality to reckon with. Her heart spoke louder than her looks and *that* was most important.

Three of the father's friends, Buckingham, Cateliffe and Nay-Smith had known Cynthia for years and had the duty to care for her and take her out, but not on a date, per se. *Three men on a date would surely crowd any young lass!*

One day, the Threescore (as she liked to call them), took Cynthia on a day visit to the Aquarium. It was exuberantly hot, as the summer sun was burning bright, through fiery windows, which absorbed its light. The little group had a wander around the smaller exhibitions. Neptune's Diamond shone brilliantly in the middle of the room, illuminating mosaic-tiled stained glass windows some bright spark had invented, as part of the exhibition. A trident rose majestically from its pedestal in glorified gold. Other artefacts collected from the sea ranged from shipwreck debris, to rock formations any self-respecting woman would love to have round her neck in jewelled form. Other rooms had tiled portraits of navigators and seamen, along with underwater landscapes and portraits of fish of many colours. Mercaste likenesses hung along a wall, were seen with dazzling interest. No regular Mortal would think these 'people' were fish... they looked like just you and me.

The Threescore and their lady had rested in the *triclinium* (the dining area), where they had some wine and beer that went with nibbles of nuts, fruit and honey-flavoured bread. They reclined on the sofas surrounding a low-lying table and relaxed for a bit, with slaves fanning them (and other customers), by their side. The men of the group were stricken with sweat-laden tunics, for they could not cope well in the heat. The rest afforded them temporary comfort and cooling. *The facilities at the Aquarium were quite convenient, indeed!* Cateliffe and Nay-Smith blasted their way through their snacks, whilst Buckingham took his approach more gingerly, as did Cynthia, who found it funny to watch these men, teeming with enthusiasm at *their* age.

Buckingham watched Cynthia, piling away at her honey-bread snack. 'You almost done yet?'

'Hang about, nearly there,' she answered, as she caught a glimpse of a familiar face in the distance.

Cateliffe also had noticed, not letting the moment pass by. 'Isn't that Mr Pymbrush?'

'Nanlee,' Cynthia called out and waved at him.

He saw the dear girl, acknowledging her with a return wave. 'Ah, hello there. Just a moment.'

Pymbrush came over to the table and sat on the corner of the sofa where Cynthia was sitting.

'How is everybody? Damnably hot, you know,' he burrowed his hand in his pocket where he found a cloth and patted the sweat off his face.

'We are all fine, just a tad warm,' Nay-Smith interjected.

'A tad warm?' Pymbrush had noticed the sweat increasing at the back of Nay-Smith's tunic. 'Now, that is an understatement!'

Nay-Smith took no notice, as he took the heat for granted and already had gotten used to the permeating perspiration.

'I'll have this washed in no-time,' he said, staring at Cynthia, who usually helped with household laundry.

Pymbrush laughed. 'I see. Enjoying the exhibition? I helped put it together, you know.'

'Did you, now,' Cateliffe responded, 'I thought I noted a flair of your contribution.'

'Thank you,' Pymbrush went on, 'We have something really special in the tanks today. We collected a great many fish for the Circus, which also includes a few Mercastes among them.'

Buckingham rang out, 'Mercastes? I thought they were mythological.'

'Like the Centaurii of the Southern Regions? Nah, we've got them in,' Pymbrush confirmed.

'They make for excellent transport, you know,' Cateliffe admitted, 'In my youth, I rode one, and they were more reliable than a horse.'

Nay-Smith perked up. 'How?'

'One can speak to them... like a chariot driver or something of the sort. Makes for good personal transport.'

'Ha-ha,' Buckingham scoffed, 'Our fair home has many odd creatures about, on land and sea.'

Pymbrush took his jovial turn, 'And we shall see those from the sea. We've captured males and females of the Mercaste species.'

'We must see these creatures for ourselves,' Cynthia added, with excitement.

Cateliffe took Pymbrush aside, 'Will we see them in action?'

Pymbrush got the hint and grinned, 'No, I am afraid not. They are disoriented outside their natural habitat and temporarily inhibited. Once they return to the open waters, they shall thrive as usual. As we clean the Circus daily, the fish have the freedom to swim away to continue their lives... then, we capture a fresh batch to view the following day.'

'No time to waste, then,' Buckingham agreed, 'You ready, Cynthia?'

She sipped the last of her drink. 'Yes, I am most eager for this.'

Pymbrush rubbed his hands. 'Splendid. You shall not be disappointed. *Post meridiem tuum est* (meaning 'the afternoon is yours'). We close at six and I will be free for dinner this evening, if you would have me.'

Cynthia's eyes sprouted a bright brown colour, as if receiving a pet. She turned to her elders, 'May I? I surely would love that.'

Buckingham would not allow his influence to mar the young girl's chances. 'You may sup with him, as long as you return at a reasonable hour.'

Cateliffe added, 'And we shall warm some milk for your nightcap.'

'Rather!' Cynthia exclaimed. She hugged Pymbrush and thanked him.

'That settles it,' Pymbrush declared, 'I will pick you up at the Square outside. Do enjoy your time here. Must dash for now.'

He hurried away from the table to his office to finish his day's work.

'Well, well, well, aren't we growing up fast,' Nay-Smith chortled.

She retorted, 'Don't you wish me to?'

'It is like having three fathers with you,' Cateliffe explained. 'We will have to let you go, one day; your father would have wanted it.'

'I do appreciate you looking after me. I hate being alone and you give good security,' she reflected.

'With that in mind, let's join the Circus.' Buckingham led the group on to the next phase of the day.

CHAPTER III

The Circus was a huge room, with dim, transparent glass surrounding all who came in. The soft mix of blue and purple gave a wisp of light, enough to watch fish tails swish away in the water. As the fish were fed for the afternoon run, no one tried to eat one another and were *tolerably* behaved.

The Mercastes swam freely and kept to the discipline of performing and conformed, usually, to the Mortal's whims. We understood what was expected of us, whereas the other fish in the tank, who hid amongst the scenery displays within, kept their agony burners alive and screamed for release back to the open sea. Truly, it felt very lonely for some of them, and as I had encountered, the results were certainly present.

As for me, I spent my confinement just swimming and swimming. I had a decent meal and stayed polite to the Mortal that fed me. I did not take offence to him, for he was only doing his job. However, I dared not speak to him, as for the moment, I was only a mere commodity of a larger exhibition. My fellow Mercastes stayed silent and we did not interact much. In the open sea, the situation was different, but I usually was alone. The old life took its toll on me and nothing would console the ache I had inside.

I swam around the fake decor and smiled to myself, thinking about the Mortal's attempt for us to 'make ourselves at home'. I knew better, of course, having seen a *real* shipwreck and fully aware of the debris these former hulks of the sea left behind. The prizes were a stunning feature of a shipwreck, but as I had no need for them, I left them to be discovered by someone else.

Through the watery glass, I saw crowds of people walking around the Circus to watch us with fascination. These exhibitions were very popular, as the fish changed daily. If one misses a day, it would be lucky for one to encounter the same fish twice.

I saw some people writing in their notebooks... *fish-spotters*, I reckoned, probably tabulating every one of us, then going to their friends to brag, 'I've seen more than you have', etc. Either that, or it could be statistical tabulation... *a census, maybe?* That is the problem of once being human... sophisticated thought sometimes clashed with beautiful simplicity. Yet, it was all a show and for show and no different from when I worked in the Amphitheatre.

Sometimes Mortals would peer closely into the tank, past the watery blur. Water had a funny way of disguise, other times, it was like having an open curtain in the evening with the lights on in the room. *Ewwuh*, it made me cringe, just thinking about that. This once happened to me, as one time, I got busy, a self-inflicted following had appeared at the window of my dressing room, peering in, just afore an evening performance... in winter. *AUGH!* For much of the time, Mortal faces were blurred; and the blur went *both* ways. I found it difficult to make out facial features or to whom I should wave, in case one had done so.

But on *this* day, something unexpected happened to me. A face had emerged more clearly than the others. I could see that she was not the ex-wife or the daughter. *Phew!* It was, however, a young lady, well of age, and certainly no child. She wore a sleeveless red top with a grey skirt, her hair flowed nicely over her shoulders, her face was round, small nose, and overall small in stature. I noticed a smile on her face... *had she seen me?* She put her hand on the tank, but for a second, which left an imprint that later caused my dominating curiosity about *her*. Her child-sized handprint had inflamed my senses and stirred me out of my secluded mentality. *I had wondered about that hand size*. The handprint lingered and I swam closer to get a better look, despite the watery distortion. She stayed where she was and I saw her through my lucid imagination; *at least the handprint was real...*

... and what a handprint it was! I had a good look at it, despite the watery distortion I had to fight. It was a diminutive size, I confirmed; of course, *that* did not matter to me, as I glanced at my hand to find a bit of webbing had grown between my fingers, resulting from all the time I had spent underwater. However, the size of her hand intrigued me... from what I saw of her, she was not a child... *so what of that size, then?* I figured it had to be some sort of accident, either from birth or during her life, being the cause of the hindrance. I carried on swimming near that handprint, shrugging off any doubt I had about this young person. I had hoped she would still be watching me, as well as the other fish, doing their acrobatic stunts to heighten the crowd's interest.

I searched the transparency to find she was still in the Circus, just in another section, gazing at the other specimens. I made my way towards her...

* * * * * *

'Look at all the beautiful fish about,' Cateliffe remarked in awe.

'They collect many species here,' Buckingham explained, 'Truly, this is a spectacular exhibition. I must congratulate Mr Pymbrush on this achievement.'

Nay-Smith noticed a tranced look upon Cynthia's face, as she stared into the deep blue water of the tank. 'You alright, girl?'

She came to very quickly. 'Um, yes. I am fine, thank you.'

Cateliffe enquired, 'Are you fancying the Mercastes, perchance?'

'Ah, just looking, really,' she denied, for she did not wish to speak of the one who caught her eye, and I, her handprint.

Fleeting motions had passed the group in the tank. My sparkling beauty had made Cynthia's companions rather suspicious.

'That one there is really remarkable,' Buckingham admitted.

If I had heard that, I would have acknowledged a thank you.

'A pretty-boy fish, if ever I saw one,' Nay-Smith agreed.

An hour had passed and the group wandered thorough the Circus fully and almost ready to depart.

'I've a date with Mr Pymbrush,' Cynthia spoke up, 'We're to meet up at the square at six.'

'You should get changed first,' Cateliffe suggested, 'And get that fish smell off you.'

'I do not smell like fish,' she protested, 'Besides, fish smells do not penetrate through glass.'

'If it could be invented, one will find a way,' Cateliffe smirked.

She continued to pout, as they went home and Cynthia prepared for her date with Pymbrush.

Damn, I could not get her attention... *must try for another opportunity.*

* * * * * *

Cynthia left her companions and headed for the Olive-Reed Square, where a sun-dial clock read, with the sun's piercing eye, a few minutes to six.

Although it was evening, the sky remained a bright blue, with a few wispy clouds kept in the distance. She sat down on the bench and waited, slightly nervous, but not agonised. Pymbrush was a decent sort and wished no harm upon anyone. He had a few prior experiences and found most women either dull, aggressive, or hardly attuned to his dapper nature, (as they found him too fussy). Yet, this is just what attracted Cynthia to him and she enjoyed his jollity, politeness and appreciated his prim sense of being...

What ho! Look at that lively gentleman heading my way, she thought. Pymbrush, in his precision, was smack on the dot and she swooned in her seat. He had a smart, but plain, linen tunic, with golden laced boots. His hair was combed back, trimmed well at the edges, which framed an eager, clean-shaven face. *One look at him would set the bells ringing.*

'Hello there, my lass,' he addressed, kissing her hand.

'Mr Pymbrush,' she answered, unabashed.

'It's Nanlee... do remember, ol' girl.'

Cynthia preferred to address her fellow in a formal manner, but as they grew familiar, the formality was deemed a redundancy. She put her hand to her head. 'Sorry, I forgot.'

'No need, no need. I am quite used to the intense reaction of women toward me.'

She blushed with extreme power. 'You do not know the half of it.'

Nanlee put his arm around her, and held her steady. 'Shall we learn of the other half? I'll take you to a friend of mine's who's holding a dinner party.'

'Sounds good. I am famished,' she agreed and got up from the bench.

'Yes, I am too. Hard day at work, and all that,' Nanlee sighed.

'At least the evenings cool off somewhat.'

He hailed a *lectica*, (which was a litter), to take him to the villa, located on a hill overlooking the Newbri Valley.

Nanlee began the conversation. 'So, what did you think of the exhibition?'

'Well displayed,' Cynthia replied, 'I enjoyed the Circus very much, especially the Mercastes included in the tank.'

'It should be changed by now, and all the beings you saw today will be sent back to the open sea. That is how I planned it.'

'I see,' she reflected, thinking about that handprint which would have been wiped off by this time. She sighed, further thinking about the Mercaste that took her eye and interest in her handprint.

Nanlee stared at her with concern. 'Are you alright? You look downcast. I thought you were happy to be with me.'

'One of the Mercastes saw me and swam my way.'

'Don't take it personally, my love. The interest goes both ways. They are keen about us, as much as we are keen on them.'

She swallowed hard. 'But this one was different. It felt as if he wanted to introduce himself.'

'Well, we do keep track of the sea life around the region, so if there was someone you wanted to see again, I could arrange this for you... and only for you.'

Cynthia gasped, 'You would do this for me?!'

'I can arrange for this Mercaste to return to the Circus, but that would be luck of the draw. We could go on an expedition to their colony on Clunia, where we could find this fellow you're after.'

'I just wanted to know why this Mercaste took a shine to me,' she uttered.

'Well, they all do,' he assured, 'That is their nature.'

The conversation paused, when Nanlee asked, 'Did you do anything special to invite the Mercaste's attention toward you?'

'I left a handprint,' she confessed.

'You did WHAT? One is not supposed to touch the glass, my dear girl.'

'I did not know this and I apologise for the transgression.' She started to cry, realising her desire to meet this Mercaste would draw her attention away from Nanlee.

Oddly, he showed no sign of jealousy nor resentment. 'Forgiven, love. I will see what I can do.'

Could this be a personal thing, or should she not take it personal in the first place? She waited for Nanlee to give her opportunity.

They reached the villa by the quickest slave runner and entered the lush grounds, where they wiled away the evening together.

CHAPTER IV

Late that night, I found myself in the ocean again, along with the others. I swam around to re-orient myself to the newness of open-aired sea. I caught glimpses of the fish who complained bitterly the previous day, with regard to their capture. Families, once fragmented, were reunited and the cries of 'Mummy, Daddy' had resonated in the depths. They said it as if they really *meant* it, and their relief was heartfelt.

I went towards a group of Mercastes sitting on a rock bed chatting away amongst themselves. I was dead nervous about going up to greet them, much less than to enquire about that diminutive Mortal girl with the handprint that caught my eye. I suffered in pain thinking about it; I decided just to wave hello and swim away... *the coward that I was!*

I continued in my solitude, going through undersea trenches, trying to find that shipwreck I spotted some time ago. The huge liner soon loomed in front of me and created a shadow which covered the immediate area in darkness. Above the grand shadow, I saw an even grander light. *This could not be...* the light would not remain constant underwater, yet it was a strange, glowing and shadowy light.

I hurried closer to find it was Neptune Himself, towering over me and the surrounding area.

'Hello, my son,' He bellowed.

The waves hit me hard with the sound of His voice.

'Ah, hello,' I answered nervously.

'I see all is not well with my flock.'

'Just a touch of the disorientation from the Circus, sir.'

'By the unholy land mass above us, damn those pesky Mortals! When will they ever learn to leave well enough alone,' He moaned.

It now occurred to me that my fellow fish were not the only ones disturbed by the Circus.

'The Mortals seek us for understanding and scientific research,' I guessed.

'Scientific research?! 'Tis exploitation of our species to you and me, lad,' He shouted.

He was most displeased.

'We were treated humanely, sir.'

'Pish and tosh... humanely... bah! The word *human* may be within the word, but that is all I will give it for. They populate my waters with rejects from their society, yourself included, and then they scoop everyone up into a huge storage tank to be put on show for Mortality. My cousin, Poseidon, also harbours a similar bane.'

'Humans are odd creatures, as you well know, and I have accepted the Kiss you have given me, my Master,' I stated.

'Yes, I have Kissed you, all right; let me check on it.'

Neptune came down from His pedestal to examine the Mark left upon my neck. He touched the area to feel the gills that have now formed there. I felt an odd sensation.

'Your breathing well down here? I knew it would be a shock; at least the gills are working properly,' He said.

I touched the gills. 'I can breathe down here, as I did on land.'

'Well, too much air in the lungs will make you go funny, yes?'

I thought that might be an issue, but as of yet, I had not inhaled air since my off-land departure.

'I reckon so, sir,' I agreed, dimly.

Neptune went sceptical on me. 'You do not seem sure. Come on, out with it. I do spare time for My children.'

I let out a sigh and Neptune sat next to me, sprawling out, as if he were reclining on a Roman sofa. He deeply gazed into my eyes.

'It's a girl, I bet, and she is not your ex-wife,' He guessed.

I could hardly keep up with godly intelligence, but I had to confess He *was* correct...

... and I spilled the beans. 'I saw a sweet looking girl, small in size and shape, who left her little handprint on the tank. It has been most likely cleaned off by now and I am all a-fuss'd over her.'

'A handprint, small or not, does not make marriages, you know,' Neptune wisely intoned.

'As you are Master of the Seas, could you help me find this girl?'

'How in water could I, Master of the Seas (as you put it), seek out a mere land-based Mortal?! Do you realise I have many creatures to look after? I do not have time for a *Mortal*. Besides, what if your sweet is married, eh? Or is she too young? Is she of age; if so, maybe with a male companion already? You do not know and there is no chance I will be able to find out.'

I hung my head low. 'Neptune, Master, I beseech thee to give it a go. She looks young, and possibly naive, but I do not believe she is a child, despite the distortion I encountered in the tank.'

'The worth of a tank's view is as blurry as you can get. I gather you must really love her that much. Remember, you have just been divorced and exiled into the sea. This yearn could just be you wanting your wife back, but as it is not your wife, then *any* woman will do. If you are desperate for a companion, I recommend befriending the other Mercastes. Perhaps they could be what you need, no?'

My eyes welled with sadness and tears would have come, if not for being underwater.

'No, sir, I want this Mortal,' I resolved, with sorrow.

'It looks like you must pay another visit to that Aquarium,' Neptune suggested.

'Good heavens,' I begged desperately, 'Please help me find her. Your omnipotence would surely help me.'

His face remained stony. 'I shall not interfere with the lives of My children.'

'But I was sent here as an outcast.'

'Yes, and now, under My jurisdiction, you are a Mercaste, and thus My child. But, it is *your own* life you live; I cannot do that for you.'

Neptune embraced me.

I asked, with a continued queasy feeling. 'So, I should go?'

'That will be your first step. When the Mortals suck up a portion of My realm, make certain you are there.'

I shook His hand and swam away. Nervously, I spent the night, deep in prayer, thinking about that girl who left a completely different mark upon me.

By morning, I searched for any suctions in the sea and other distortions indicating Mortal activity. I tried to look my best, but when one was beneath the sea, looks did not matter. The female Mercastes, of course, retained their natural cared-for beauty; *it must be the salt in the water*.

I glided along the bottom, seeking refreshment from some smaller creatures whose sole purpose was to be eaten. Truly, I had forgotten what a *proper* meal tasted like. I so missed the life I once lived on land, as a Mortal. My mind began to remember things and meditated about them... one of which was, *who took over my duties at the Amphitheatre?*

I was thinking about my previous existence, when I was interrupted by a whirring sound and a swirly hole emerged in the water. *Good graces, they're at it again!* I took dear Neptune's advice and stayed close to the entity. I let myself be absorbed by the rush and braced myself as I had done before. Soon, I was returned to that jolly great fish tank of the Circus.

Ah yes, I remember now... my fellow sea creatures flipping the distortion out of their systems, others bemoaned their fate, and the younger folk whinged about being separated from family. I felt sorry for this lot, and personally wondered who was looking after my children. It was a sad moment, but I sacrificed my emotion to adhere to the task at hand, which was to find that girl.

So, I made myself lively, in case I get lucky and she happened to be there. I saw an increasing crowd, and looked frantically for that young girl with the mysterious handprint.

CHAPTER V

Nanlee Q. Pymbrush came into work that morning. His supervisor, Raybin, was waiting for him in his office.

'I want a word with you, Pymbrush,' he said sternly.

'Right-o,' Nanlee answered, coming into his office.

'I've got word that someone left a handprint on the tanks in the Circus. You need to be more vigilant; we cannot have the sea life go barmy on us,' Raybin chastised.

Nanlee stood up. 'Mr Raybin, sir, I am doing all I can to make the fish feel at home and I do discourage public infringement upon their safety. I am aware of this handprint, for it was my friend Cynthia who left it. She put her hand on the tank to attract a Mercaste who took interest in her.'

'See that no further attraction continues, Pymbrush. These creatures are now fish, and no longer one of us. Do remember that, lad.'

He walked out in a huff. Nanlee slumped in a chair and sighed. He kept a silence for a minute or so, either to calm down or say a prayer (one could not determine which). Without Cynthia around, how was he to help her locate the special Mercaste? He would not know which one to remove from the tank. He thought about what Raybin had said, and yes, he was correct, *but in affairs of the heart, the superior was dead wrong.*

Nanlee walked into the main exhibition room where the Circus was placed and searched the tank for the Mercastes the Aquarium had captured that day. Out of character and in sight of a group of Mercastes, he put his own handprint on the glass, hoping it would attract the being in question...

... but would it work?

* * * * * *

I was listening with earnest to a fish who had lost his way and was lonely for companionship. We talked for some time when I glanced at the water's edge. I saw a familiar entity... *the handprint!*

I excused myself from the conversation to take a closer look. It was a handprint, but not *the* handprint. It was too big. The one I remembered was diminutive.

Suddenly, I noticed a waving action from within the crowd. I followed the motion, but I was no fool. There was hesitation in my motion, as I slowly realised this wave was coming from a *man*. This Mortal was signalling me toward a secluded exit point, where I hoisted myself out of the tank, or tried to anyway. It was difficult to climb with the lower fin, but I did the best I could, with the Mortal's help. Upon breathing fresh air, I exhaled wildly, as it rushed into my lungs was fast as water would when I dove into the sea.

And what a breath that was! By the gods, I had forgotten how good it felt.

I was carried into a back room by two men, one of whom had a remarkable resemblance to myself. It was a vision of a mirror image that I had not seen since the day of my exile, after the divorce. I stirred my mind to awaken to what was happening to me, as now that I was breathing *air*, it was my turn to be disoriented.

The men had taken me to a table to lay me out on and dry me off. Towels were placed on my lower non-human region, and I took a towel and helped quicken the process.

The man, similar in face, asked, 'Can you speak?'

'Of course, I can,' I retorted, 'I am not inept and certainly not an animal of any sort!'

'No need to get uptight; do calm down, please,' the 'twin' answered.

I sucked in a breath, but I felt slight animosity toward the situation. 'Where the hell am I anyway and who are you?'

The other man excused himself, leaving the look-alike alone with me.

'My office. I say, you look like a sacred twin,' the fellow marvelled, drawing near to me, then introduced himself. 'I'm Nanlee Q. Pymbrush. I do research for the Aquarium.'

'How do you do. I am Alexander Nespor, former thespian.'

We shook hands.

'Ah, you are one of those actor-chappies from the Amphitheatre, then?'

'I was, until I was sent to the deep.'

Nanlee looked concerned. 'What happened?'

'Marital troubles. I am sorry, but I do not wish to relay anything further, please.' I lowered my head.

He put his hand upon my shoulder. 'Is it like that?'

I shed a tear, *at last*. 'Worse, thank you.'

'Dear me,' Nanlee paused, 'And now to business. The reason I took you out of the tank is that a young lady is just dying to meet you.

'She is a good friend of mine and the one responsible for the handprint that possibly wound you up.'

I perked up considerably. 'Who... who is she?'

'Like I said, she is a good friend of mine named Cynthia.'

Ah, so that's who it was...

'Are you close to her?'

Nanlee pondered. 'We went out the previous evening together... to a party a close friend gave at his villa. I want to further the conquest.'

Do you now?? Ggrrrrr...

'She is a small package of loveliness,' he added.

I would have made a fist and later, made a break for it, but thought better, as by now, I was quite indecent at the moment.

I enquired. 'Do you have any spare clothing?'

'I think there is something in the Lost and Found section which had not been claimed for some time that you can wear. I'll go and fetch it.'

Nanlee left the room and I remained on the table. I saw that my legs and feet had reformed, and I gazed at them, as if for the first time, as a baby would. I tried to leave the table to walk a bit, but I wobbled too much and grabbed the table's edge, fighting to remain stood up.

He soon returned with a garment when he assisted me. 'Would you like a chair?'

'Yes,' I gasped.

Nanlee went to the other side of the room and grabbed a chair. He helped me onto it.

'Now, here is a tunic that you may wear to cover up. We usually do not entertain a fish, much less an ex-human, so our needs would not cater for one.'

'It is good enough.' I struggled to lower the tunic over myself, Nanlee continued to assist me. 'I am most grateful.'

'Not at all. It's for my friend... just to quench her curiosity.'

My interest in Cynthia was now bordering on the more-than-curious, and the sooner I met her, the better.

'Can you stand up and walk? I am willing to help you all I can, but I shan't carry you,' Nanlee said.

Since being in the chair, I felt helpless, realising infantile ability with regard to walking. I got up anyway, with Nanlee holding me, and took my first steps.

I looked at him. 'You know, I prefer swimming to walking.'

'It's probably an acquired taste.'

'Not a bad one, once you get used to it. You should try swimming.'

'I'm not much of a swimmer, though I do know how. It's a requirement for the job.'

'Your research takes you into Neptune's realm?'

'Could be, if needed. There are others who are strictly divers and they do most of the tabulations.'

'I see.' I still felt downcast.

'You look like you could use something. I've got just the thing.'

Nanlee fiddled in a draw and took out a bottle of wine that seemed to be saved for a latter day.

'Fresh from the Newbri Valley,' he boasted.

'Good vintage?'

'A '57.'

'Not bad. I like the '69 better.'

Goblets were retrieved from the shelves and we imbibed. It was most refreshing... I only wished this Cynthia would be here to share the drinks with us. *Damn damn damn!*

I wanted to know more about the girl. 'So, how long have you known her?'

'A few years, though it feels like I've known her forever. We've dated on and off, but my research takes opportunity away, if you see my point.'

'I confess to you, that was the reason for my divorce. Too much work and the wife's heart...'

'... wandered about,' he finished the sentence. 'Cynthia understands my work and need for the fish's welfare.'

'Did you ever try to propose?'

'Time was unkind toward that end,' Nanlee reflected, sadly, 'It seems though that she could be more interested in you, for some reason. Could be why she left her handprint, I guess.'

He guessed... humph! 'As you took the trouble to release me from the sea, I really want to meet her.'

'And so you shall, but I do not know when she'll be coming by today.'

'You are actively dating the lady; doesn't she come round to your office?'

'Sometimes, when planned, though. She usually stays with her companions.'

Companions? This was a shock.

Nanlee saw my perturbed countenance. 'I would not worry. They are her father's friends. They have been looking after her, since her father's passing.'

I still wondered who was looking after my children.

'They do not control her life, but she feels attached to them, for some reason or other,' he continued.

'Loyalty, maybe?'

'Perhaps. By the way, would you like to stay at my place, at least until I introduce you?'

'That is most kind, thank you.' I was relieved. He did remove me from my new home, so it seemed proper for him to be responsible for my well being. *I did recall earlier something about the fish's welfare*??!!

Nanlee noticed the Kiss on my neck. 'Did you injure yourself?'

'No,' my hand reached for the spot, 'It is called Neptune's Kiss and one receives this when they are committed to the sea.'

'Wow,' he gaped.

We stared at one another.

'Call me Alec.'

'Nanlee,' he smiled.

We shook hands again.

'You know, Alec, we really do look alike.'

'Only a belch of the gods, pay no mind,' I dismissed.

'We could be the twins of the stars.'

I mocked the notion. 'Pastor and Bollux?'

We laughed vigorously.

Nanlee stopped laughing. 'I could be mistaken for you and be thrown into the tank, you know.'

'If the sandal fits...'

'Oh, never mind.'

I remained in Nanlee's office until completion of his hard day's work... *then it will be time to meet Cynthia.*

CHAPTER VI

I waited in Nanlee's office all afternoon. The sands of time dripped slowly by, and I just stared out into oblivion... not knowing where I would be in the next moment, or what. It was a distasteful experience, being thrown out of one world and into another. Then to be suddenly cast out again, returning to the world of the Mortals, was just *too much!* My thoughts were precariously close to utter boredom and for a former Mortal like myself, it proved hard to bear... much more than I realised.

I noticed the door was slightly left ajar, and I figured Nanlee would be returning shortly, so I did not close it fully. Yet, I was rudely intruded by someone who turned out not to be Nanlee.

'Hello,' I called out.

'Pymbrush?' The voice was unfamiliar, slightly intimidating and certainly *not* Nanlee.

The newcomer barged his way in, looking for Nanlee, when he saw me and totally flipped out of his mind, shouting, 'What in Hades' hole are you doing here? Visitors are unauthorised in these offices. You are trespassing, sir.'

'I am here at Mr Pymbrush's request. I was told to remain here, for I have a meeting with someone.'

He snidely retorted, 'Oh, do you now?'

I got scared.

So scared...

... that I...

The man examined me within my proximity. 'What is that mark you've got on your neck?'

I touched the Kiss I was given when cast into the sea. 'Oh, it's an old injury,' I lied.

Realisation dawned upon the most ugliest day. 'You are a Mercaste, aren't you?'

'I, umm......,' I could not find the words to defend myself. I froze as foreign prey.

'Wait a minute,' the man recalled, 'You're that actor fellow who was sent below. And below is where you will remain.'

He suddenly grabbed me, as I tried to make haste toward the door. He was too fast for me (impressive for a late middle-aged one), and a scuffle broke out. I was nearly set free, when passing Aquarium staff, (originally minding their *own* business, mind you), joined in and had me tied down.

'You are a flipping fish,' the man exclaimed. He turned to the two staff members. 'You two, put him back into the tank.' He went into another room.

I was disrobed from my given tunic and laid out naked to be returned to the Circus, when Nanlee turned up to find me in distress.

'I say, wait,' Nanlee shouted, 'I need him for experimentation.'

One of the two quipped, 'We are to return him to the tank.'

Nanlee remained firm, and not amused. 'Well, I am telling you, as your superior to release him to me, as he is imperative to my work.'

'You have no authority over us.'

Nanlee stood his ground and stared hard at them in an uncharacteristically aggressive manner.

They relented and let go their nasty grip upon me, losing the battle and walking away. Nanlee retained his bulldog stance all the while...

... however that dodgy fellow, who gate-crashed my peace in the office, came up to him...

... and shouted green blood. 'PYMBRUSH!'

'Raybin,' Nanlee growled, his eyes reflecting his newfound toughness.

'You removed a fish out of the tank without authorisation. Do you know what this means,' Raybin chastised.

Nanlee scoffed thumbtacks back at him, maintaining a veiled innocence. 'Umm... it means we have one less fish for display, amongst the hundreds we have already. Anyway, I need this one for experimentation.'

'Experimentation?! Sod your bleeding experimentation. One less fish means less to show. People pay good money to us to showcase these many species, especially the Mercastes.'

Nanlee continued the pout and anger slowly built a skyscraper within him. Raybin also kept his uncaring bearing, spitting forth counter-emotion that threatened to crash into it.

'Take the Mercaste back to the tank now, or your job is on the line!'

Raybin stomped away, like a one way steam funnel that never went anywhere.

Nanlee looked at me in despair. 'I am so sorry, so sorry, ol' boy.' He started to weep for me and the disappointment that awaited with regard to Cynthia.

'I know, Nanlee.' I gave him a hug. 'This can wait awhile. Let it blow over. Another time, perhaps. Be calm first.'

'For a Mercaste, you are most wise.'

'Hades, I have dealt with things like this before... bitchy wife comes to mind.'

'Not as bad as bitchy boss.'

Nanlee grimaced at the situation when he glanced at my body. 'You are naked, you know.'

'I have been disrobed. Get me back into that tank, quickly. I will be alright.'

I led him to the inevitable.

'Another day,' I said.

'Goodbye, Alec.'

'Faretheewell,' I gulped in one breath, 'We will meet shortly. Seek out that girl amongst the Mortal party and tell her what happened. I must speak to Neptune again... I shall be tanked no longer!'

Nanlee had a blank moment, when he realised there *was* faith underwater. It certainly made for a stimulating anthropological discussion, IF he was able to interview me further.

'I will tell her.'

I opened the portal and climbed back into my watery world. I swam away and my fin formed once again. Through the glass, I seized Nanlee's attention and signalled a thumbs-up, to which he responded with a wave. I saw a tear racing down the path of his face and I knew a better plan was needed to meet Cynthia.

* * * * * *

I swam in familiar territory again, as my lungs filled with water and expelled it out, creating a group of bubbles. The gills were working at peak time, and it felt nice to be home again... *but not under such horrid circumstances.*

The day wore on and soon I caught a glimpse of something or someone I had seen before...

The girl...

I went straight to the pane of the tank.

Oh yes, oh yes! It was that girl with the handprint!

I began to feel enthusiasm, as the earlier clash with Nanlee's superior was thankfully forgotten. I did flips around the tank and experienced a vigour I had not displayed since my early theatre days.

Outside, someone in the crowd commented, 'That Mercaste seems most lively. I wonder what's revving his engines up?'

Another spectator, next to him, said, 'Ah, it's just for show, I'm certain. Naught to be worried about. This is what we pay good denarii for.'

Cynthia had then appeared and approached the tank, putting her face close up. I now finally got to read through the spongy mist of water, and see distinction in her face.

I definitely liked what I saw. Child-like looks complimented her demeanour and she seemed to have spirit. I waved my fin at her and she giggled in response. I gave her a personal show of myself (not unlike what I did as an actor), flipping and swirling around, enjoying the moment immensely. I really wanted to give her joyous time to remember fondly.

Suddenly, I noticed someone in the crowd had seen my antics and moved toward Cynthia. *Was this person one of those companions Nanlee referred to?*

'Cynthia, pay no mind to this. Do not forget, they are just fish.'

'This one is surely excitable and seems pleased to see me, Buckingham.'

'Yes,' Cateliffe remarked, 'And we are not allowed to over excite them.'

Nay-Smith came over to the little group. 'He's a fish, a flipping mad fish. He is not one of us.'

'But, he was... once. And I think I love him,' she swooned.

'Not anymore. He belongs in the tank or in the sea. There is no place for him around us, and certainly not around *you*,' Buckingham argued.

'You never have interfered with whom I chose to date. I do not see what the problem is,' Cynthia pouted.

'Your dates are usually Mortal beings, yes? Why on earth would you want to date a *fish*, when you can have me,' Cateliffe offered.

'Ummm...,' she hesitated. 'I like you but cannot see myself on a date with you. You're like a father to me.'

'A father, unrelated,' Cateliffe confirmed.

She threw her hands up in agony. 'He looks so happy. Why the mystery? What have you got against him?'

Buckingham saw a rough nerve emerge, touched by the armada of emotions, which he felt should not be on public display.

'We have nothing against fish. In fact, they are quite tasty when seasoned upon a plate for dinner.'

Cynthia was overwrought and slapped Buckingham hard on the cheek. Her eyes showed defiance and was unimpressed by his view on sea life.

Buckingham took offence at this. 'You, young lady, are now leaving these premises. Furthermore, you are grounded.'

'But I am of age, I do not have to listen to you,' she ranted.

'Cateliffe, take the dear girl to the chariot and send her home, *accompanied*,' Buckingham ordered.

'But...,' she struggled weakly and was led away by Cateliffe.

'Maybe you will change your mind about me,' he sniggered.

They left the Aquarium, leaving Buckingham and Nay-Smith reflecting on her actions. They, too, were bombarded with a similar armada of emotions... which they never recalled ever feeling before in their many-odd years of life between them.

That same armada came upon me too, through the waters of the tank. I decided to stay away from being too close to the crowd and let the buggers marvel at some *other* delight. My heart broke and I was deeply hurt by the Mortal's actions against my Cynthia, despite my never having met her... *yet*. Although I could not hear clearly what was going on between her and the men who stood by her, it did not take a Plato to figure out why they took her away from me.

So, I remained, hidden behind the underwater decor until the suction-into-the-sea sent me away from this devastating place. When the time came, later that evening, I gladly subjected myself to its force, to be expelled back into the mystical open sea.

At last, I found my release and I made way toward the Clunian shoreline to take in the cool evening that awaited...

CHAPTER VII

Buckingham and Nay-Smith stayed at the Circus to seek the proprietor to make a complaint. Thankfully, Nanlee was still on site, working his final minutes. He was walking toward his office to finish off the day.

Buckingham's stern voice echoed, 'Mr Pymbrush?'

Nanlee turned around. 'Ah, Bucks, old chap. How are you?'

'Don't Bucks me... are you aware a Mercaste has taken interest in our Cynthia and that she has fallen for him?'

Nanlee paused and was unsure whether to tell Buckingham the full situation.

Nay-Smith interjected, 'We believe she is in love with your *fishy* exhibition.'

'Right,' Nanlee acknowledged, with a tinge of embarrassment.

'We've sent her home with Cateliffe,' Buckingham said, 'And she is grounded. So, what are you going to do about it?'

Nanlee disagreed with the clash of opinion. 'That is a bit harsh, I'd say. She is an *adult*, you know.'

'It is not that,' Nay-Smith frowned, 'But she is budding herself toward a *fish* and we do not wish for her to be harmed by this.'

''Tis no harm in this, surely,' Nanlee scoffed, 'The more we research and get to know these creatures, the less we are a-feared of them.'

'I do not care about your blasted research,' Nay-Smith yelled.

'These creatures were once Mortals with different stories, but the point is, they are outcasts from our society, for whatever reason and the reason is usually a bad one,' Buckingham argued. 'We do not want her among that element.'

Nanlee was good at conjecture, and knew Cynthia and the Mercaste in question would get on, once they met. After all, the interest was there and both seemed keen on one another.

'Maybe she is better off with the fish, considering he was once the most popular actor in Pallancium,' Nanlee pondered aloud.

'I do not give a Cato if he was an actor, librarian or a space agent! This once-Mortal is now classed as an animal and definitely beneath us,' Buckingham stated.

Nanlee could not believe the ruthlessness of Buckingham's attitude, considering he'd known the fellow a long time. These views were a consternation to him.

'Oh, well, we will see about that, sir,' Nanlee defended, deciding to expel the beans of many shapes and sizes. 'In fact, I have met this *fish*, as you call him, and he is a very kind and intelligent creature.'

'Is he now?' Nay-Smith sneered.

'And he likes Cynthia,' Buckingham added.

'SO WHAT?' Nanlee raised his voice, again uncharacteristically, 'It is not his fault he was cast into the sea. He had marital problems and his wife divorced him on bitter grounds. He is extremely lonely.'

'Divorced?' Buckingham and Nay-Smith could not believe their ears.

'Yes, and he wants to meet Cynthia,' Nanlee said.

'Over our dead bodies,' Buckingham threatened.

'No need to be like that.' Nanlee tossed their attitude aside.

'Well, she is, at present, grounded until she minds her manners,' Buckingham replied.

Nanlee was crushed to hear this, but keep his stiff stance at maximum.

'I will give you a week, and call on the lady then,' Nanlee announced, then he rushed past.

He left the two men and thought that the ball was in *their* court. *Let them make the move, take it or leave it.* He humphed his way toward his office, where he gathered some items, including the discarded tunic and went home.

* * * * * *

I, on the other hand, relaxed on Clunia, when one of the other dried-off Mercastes walked over to me.

'Hi, I'm Colpert. Is this seat taken?'

I stared at the newcomer. 'Feel free, man. I'm Alec.' I laid back to continue my reverie about Cynthia.

'Good to meet you. Your face suggests a girl-on-the-mind. Care to discuss it?'

I sighed, thinking about the overbearing weight of newly discovered prejudice which emanated from Pallancium.

'They've taken someone away from me who I wanted to meet. It was arranged until some dimwit with no culture or lick of intelligence kicked off. A situation arose and I'm now here.'

'Sorry to hear that,' Colpert lamented. 'Mortals can be very limited in their thinking. One cannot imagine achievement unless you've had a full life. A life beyond the land gives better perspective. Being a fish is far superior than being a Mortal, I think.'

'It is joyless to me. I used to be well loved and cherished as part of Pallancium culture. I had a spat of difference with the wife and now I am here. Now, I believe my heart had given way elsewhere.'

'Ohh, your problems are most complicated.' Colpert looked down. 'Do you realise your business is showing?'

'Let it show, let it flow. That is what we are all about here,' I glanced at Colpert, 'I must say that you are showing too.'

'Am I? Fishscales!' Colpert cussed, racing to find a spare cloth from a Mercaste who decided to submerge.

I laid back, not caring on *how* I looked, secure in my estate, and watched the sky turn a deep blue. The moon appeared and a few stars graced the heavens. I thought about my joke with Nanlee about the twins… Pastor and Bollux. I smirked to myself and whiled my time in meditative splendour.

My caring was minimal, and nothing was to end this flow of energy.

… and I could Mortalise myself on my own terms!

The next morning, I awoke to the pitter-patter of wet feet… *can't be the children, for they're nearly grown-up by now.*

The spotty-wet feeling persisted and I opened my eyes and saw a rainstorm emerging from the Heavens.

I panicked for a second, then (before my legs gave way to the fin) I ran my nakedness into the sea. As I splashed into the water, I was most grateful that I got there in time, for I would have been carried by other Mercastes trying to escape the rain. It would have been a most embarrassing situation, and possibly a funny one to a Mortal's mind. *No doubt Nanlee would have something to research here....*

As it continued to rain above, I felt safe within the sea's grasp. I breathed through my gills and now, nothing could dampen my spirit. Despite this, I felt I needed to resolve my conflict with the Mortal world above. I went on an adventurous stroll, if one could *call* it that, and came across some oddball items left behind by previous generations of Mortals. I found it annoying to think one would see Neptune's realm as a dumping ground for unwanted items left behind from older civilisations. *Wasn't that what museums were built for?*

Well, amongst the bits of coinage and a jewel or two, I came across a bent sword. It was not a large piece, like the props I used in the theatre, but rather it was rusty and medium-sized, which could have belonged to *anyone*. Speculation was rife when it came to antiquity, so I decided to leave it to the professionals... *or the gods.*

Speaking of gods, a Light had shone in front of me, and I used it to try to make out some odd etchings done in the metalwork. It seemed hopeless, when the Light caught up with me.

'Greetings, my child of the sea,' the voice incanted.

I looked up. Neptune. *Now, what did He want?*

'Hello,' I spoke, lukewarm in my tone.

The Great god spoke, 'I have seen better responses at a fish-market. Your sound is dull. Are you not happy to see me?'

I whinged, spoiled in my posture. 'Fuckin' Mortals, Neptune! I had her... I nearly had her!'

'Now now, Alec. None of this cussing... you, of all people, should know better than that. You silly one; to whom do you refer?'

I gave Him a silent *duh* look, pointing out His omnipotence and that *He* should know in the first place.

Neptune got the gist. *He ain't daft.* 'Ah, her.'

'Yes, HER!'

'There is no sense pouting about it. Be suave; be proactive. I do it. Why can't you?'

I could hardly contain myself. 'Were you ever thwarted by Mortal bigotry? You ought to try it. It is such a scream... which is what I am about to do.'

He went all sarcastic on me. 'I am sure it is a most distasteful pleasure. However, I have had my day of confoundment.'

'I'm sure you had,' I hissed back.

'Don't take that tone with me, young man,' came the ominous reply.

I could hardly be called young.

'Well?'

'Well what?'

I spat another *humph* at Him.

Neptune gazed at me, entering my very soul. 'Paying me disrespect? After all I've done for you?'

I felt remorse. 'Alright. One should not paint fire in front of a god. I am sorry.'

'My son. Your fire had not covered the canvas, because it would be quenched the moment it reaches My border.'

This smart-arse always had an answer to everything!

Neptune read my mind's wandering folly, but forgave the incense of thought. 'Let us leave the painted fires to the masses. Tell me what's up with you.'

He opened His arms and cradled me, as if I were a child (*and I most certainly was not!*). I did confess this proved comforting. I began to inform Him of what happened at the Aquarium, my meeting with Nanlee and his removing me from the tank. Then the nasty business with his superior... *oh, what an insufferable experience I had!*

I started to sob. '... and I was so bloody happy, when Nanlee released me back into the tank... because I saw HER! I was trying to get her attention and did a show for the masses, which in turn was aimed at the girl. She was delighted at the sight of my little water acrobatics... and then...'

'And then?'

'The Mortals took exception and realised what went on. I went back to the sea and stayed overnight on Clunia. Although I could not discern the girl's situation, I am sure the effects fell upon her, too. I believe she got into trouble for it.'

'For what?'

'Her show at liking *me*. Her companions had sent her away, from what I saw through the glass. It pains me so...'

Neptune was sympathetic. 'Your earlier spat at me is truly understandable. If this happened to *Me*, the world would never breathe air again.'

'Yeah, I am sorry about all that.'

'I know you did not mean it, son.'

He gave me a hug. 'You had your sad discourse with Me; now it is time to act and get her to meet you. You must enter the Mortal's world, dressed properly. I can hide your Kiss and make it look like a scar of some kind. I can also suspend your aquatic breaths and allow you to temporarily *be* a Mortal, for a spell. Once a day, you will have to find water, a bath perhaps, and let your fin hang out.'

'I think I can handle that,' I answered, most hopeful.

'I'll have the Clunians fashion you with gear and you will have to go by boat to Pallancium. If you swim, you'll end up naked and you are back to the start. Not good. You need to become Mortal, so you have to look the part and all. A beard might help as well.'

'My lord, I was an actor in my previous life, before the cast-off.'

'Well, then this job should be a doddle to you. By the way, did you catch the girl's name?'

'It is Cynthia, who is a friend of Nanlee Q. Pymbrush, a researcher at the Aquarium.'

'Ah, so that's your Nanlee. I do recollect the name from somewhere,' He nodded.

'I've met him. He was the one who got me out of the tank, but how did you know?'

'Do not forget that I'm omnipotent and I heard you mention it earlier. I feel it is My business to know who is messing about with My realm.'

'True, they do much oceanic work.'

'Aye, they do and it is annoying to Me. I have to keep track of all My children and see to their well-being.'

I sat, pending in silence. Neptune let go of me and bade me farewell. He tended to His business and I swam away, seeking that sword I found previously.

CHAPTER VIII

Once I located the sword, I decided to carry it as a charm-piece. *Don't know why, it is just my belief in luck*, I supposed.

I returned to the above world of Clunia, where I tried to relax. After all, a meeting with a god was no easy feat. I kept the bent sword with me and in plain view, I spotted Nanlee on a boat along the shore, doing his rounds.

Thinking about my chat with Neptune, I waved at Nanlee to grab his attention. He took the bait, as it were, and waved in return. He attended to his surveying; when he finished his writing, he brought the boat closer to the island.

'Alec,' he called out, 'I'll be right over.'

I stood up and acknowledged this with a nod, until a young female Mercaste, fully human-formed, passed me by.

'Here, take this. You will need it.' She saw my rawness and gave me an old, kick-about cloth.

I thanked her and wrapped the item round my torso. The other Mercastes giggled, but ignored the issue, as they had the same problem too. They were also aware of Mr Pymbrush, and his studious activities, and went about their own business of the day.

'Here we are,' Nanlee announced, 'Is it alright to dock here?'

'There's a post a few feet away,' I pointed past the bubble-gum tree on the right, past the Benelophant Downs.

Nanlee took the boat in the direction I showed him. He then walked back to me. 'That is most good of you.' He had a look around. 'I say, this is such a nice place.'

'One has to swim to receive such a place.'

'Ah, but I sailed here,' he grinned.

'It is a place for us to recall our humanity. No one holds a grudge against the Mortal world and we expect to be seen by your people.'

'Yes, well,' Nanlee was only *too* alert about the Mortal's attitude toward Mercastes. He glanced at the bent sword I held in my grasp. 'I see you've found the sword of Efflyn.'

'I found it underneath and carry it for luck,' I replied.

'There are cast-offs of all sorts, down here, so we've found,' Nanlee explained. 'Other theories state that people try to appease a god or two and use their Mortal possessions as a sacrifice, or to remember a loved one who once owned it or some other cause. Sometimes, they think their dead *are* under the sea.'

How wrong Nanlee was about the terrors of the deep, or so it is thought. 'Mortals don't know half what is down there.'

'That is why we do research,' Nanlee quipped. 'Legend has it that Efflyn was a crude warrior, but an efficient sort. He had a brother called Aelcyn, who was a farmer more than a fighter. It is believed that Aelcyn probably threw that sword into the sea in memory of Efflyn, out of respect for an honourable death in battle.'

'Or,' I added sarcastically, 'It could be a dishonourable creation and the smith cast it out himself.'

Nanlee cracked a joke on me. 'Well, at any rate, there is plenty of water to drink, no? If you go by the legend, you can make a wish and send the sword to its watery home.'

'Alright, I'll do it.' I closed my eyes and made a wish. What should I wish for... *duh...* we all know what I want to wish for... *Cynthia!*

I threw the damn thing into the sea. It sploshed and sunk quick. I'll probably find it again another day...

... *some wish.*

Nanlee looked at me. 'Do you know what happened to Cynthia?'

'She's been taken away from me. I saw her through the Circus tank and I attracted her attention. She was quite enthralled with me and the feeling was mutual. It was a meeting of sorts, but I want to meet her properly.'

'I know and you will. I had words with her companions. I've given them a week's time, when I promised I would call on her. We can devise a plan in the meantime, so you can formally meet.'

'I had words with Neptune and *He* was unimpressed at their behaviour,' I revealed.

He was flabbergasted. 'You have access to the gods?'

'Just the one... Neptune, the Father of the Seas and we are His children, though he does not treat us *like* children. He would not baby us, for He knows we are grown adults.'

'Oh, Heaven forbid that.'

'Would you trifle with the gods, sir? I must tell you, Mr Pymbrush, Neptune knows of you and hopes you endeavour to maintain His realm with respect.'

'Don't I always? In fact, I like the idea that someone is caring for those below the sea, if not myself, of course.'

'Fish take care of themselves, but Neptune is the god for all of us, full-bodied fish and Mercaste. He's taken keen interest in the Mercaste, for it fascinates him to think a part of humanity resides within His realm.'

'Lending a dialogue between the species,' Nanlee said.

'Yes. I have spoken to a few fish during my time here, but we keep to ourselves mainly and give courtesy toward one another's space. Everyone helps one another, but it is more about instinct and common sense to us.'

'Like that girl who passed you the cloth?'

I blushed, 'Yeah, something like that... a *utilitarian* gesture.'

'You make it sound like an off-shoot religion.' Nanlee exhaled a deep sigh. 'I do want to take you to her.'

'Neptune had suspended my aquatic status to enter your society for the purpose. He is fully aware of my yearning. I can walk among your people, as long as I keep in touch with the water once a day.'

'You will require a bath, then. Private, I reckon; the public ones do not allow Mercastes. Patrons complain about the smell.'

'We Mercastes do not *smell*,' I protested.

'It's the salt and fishy air about your people.'

'I--,' I stuttered, having to silently admit to the salted air, at least.

'I'm not offended. I've got a bath in my place. You may stay the week until I get Cynthia back,' Nanlee offered. 'But I will have to disguise you. It had been some time, but I do not want to take a chance. You were very popular at the Amphitheatre, weren't you?'

'I was, but most people had forgotten about me and moved on to the next star-of-the-moment. It's like that and expected,' I scoffed.

'Let's get home and formulate a plan.' Nanlee invited me into the boat. The other Mercastes and I exchanged waves; some of them gave me extra clothing, if one could call it that. They wished me well and they, too, moved to other pastures among themselves. Some remained on Clunia, whilst others decided to take to the waters.

* * * * * *

I stayed at Nanlee's home for a week, occasionally going out, but I had to disguise myself, for fear of recognition. I was hoping my theory of celebrity amnesia would prove itself; however, I did not wish to chance it. When he worked, I remained and passed the time reading scrolls he'd written regarding his research, among others about science and philosophy. I admitted I found them boring, but his work on aquatic life proved interesting. *I believed Neptune would think so, too.* The house itself was sparse and obviously without a woman's touch. It proved mostly functional for someone who spent more time at work than at domestics.

One day, Nanlee called on Cynthia, who was only too eager to meet him again. There wasn't anything more that Buckingham, Cateliffe and Nay-Smith could do, as to further her confinement would become detrimental. *It was not the result they were after anyway.*

Nanlee was greeted at the door by Buckingham. 'Mr Pymbrush, I trust you are here to see Cynthia.'

He walked in, replying, 'I am not here to take *you* out, am I? That would look odd, don't you think?'

'Hmmm, quite odd, indeed,' Buckingham answered, excusing himself as Cateliffe came into the room.

'Can I offer you anything?'

'Erm... I'm fine, thanks,' Nanlee smiled nervously, 'Just waiting on the lass.'

'You seem very taken with her,' Cateliffe observed.

'Well, she is a treasure to me, and I do love her, if only as a friend.'

'We've resolved the schism with Cynthia, you know.'

Nanlee turned to Cateliffe. 'I am surprised at your attitude towards fish.'

'I am not against fish, Mr Pymbrush, but one does not expect the little lady to bring home a halibut to introduce us to... unless, of course, he's wrapped up well, fresh from the market.'

He tutted, 'You seem to be unaware that the fish world is more than a conglomeration in a pie. They are living and thinking beings, Mercastes especially.'

'Well, Cynthia is attracted to one, it seems, and there is no sense to further argue the matter,' Cateliffe said.

'Good,' Nanlee smiled, 'Because I plan to introduce her to him.'

Cateliffe's eyes bulged, as he backed away, calling the other two into the room.

The three companions had surrounded Nanlee, when Cynthia walked in on them.

'Is this an Adonis contest? If so, I would love to be the judge and I judge the lot of you the winners,' she exclaimed, giggling.

The men in the vicinity blushed fervently at her comment; Nanlee went up to Cynthia and embraced her.

'Sweet talk thou'ast made, for I shall have your wish forth laid,' he drivelled poetically.

A quizzical look piled upon her face. 'Huh?'

'I will introduce you to the Mercaste that caused all the fuss,' came the clarification.

'Ah, thank you,' she grabbed him and held him tight.

'See now she doesn't get hurt, mind,' Nay-Smith warned.

Buckingham prodded him. 'We've been through this before. Cynthia has a good mind and should have decorum fused into her blood by now. There shall be no further discourse, we agreed.'

'I'll be alright,' Cynthia reassured, 'I do not think it is wise to prevent one from exploring other worlds, as it will only make the curiosity far worse.'

'And Alec is about the burst at the seams over this,' Nanlee added.

'Alec?' The quizzical look became fashionable again, this time on Cateliffe.

'Mr Nespor, the player from the Amphitheatre,' Nanlee affirmed.

Buckingham thought he had a card to play here and did so happily. 'I heard that after his expulsion, his son took over and became wildly popular, with young and old audiences, the latter happy to see the torch passed on.'

Nanlee had much to reveal upon his return home....

'I guess I shall be going then,' he sighed, offering his arm, 'Cynthia?'

'Coming,' she called, and clasped to his arm.

'You have a good time now,' Buckingham said.

'We might be late, or possibly invite her to my place,' Nanlee suggested.

She pleaded, 'Can't I?'

'No sense putting our paws where they are not wanted,' Nay-Smith dismissed.

'Just be careful, Cynthia.' Cateliffe gave her a kiss. 'Still, I wish it were me.'

'Maybe you should find someone then.'

'We're past it,' Buckingham whinged.

'One is never past it, unless one has passed on,' she stated philosophically.

They left the three stunned men, and spent a pleasant evening together.

CHAPTER IX

The night passed dryly in the air, for there was no rain this time. Nanlee and Cynthia passed the time walking down a lane, leading to his small apartment... and the greatest prize which awaited... *me*.

He opened the door to find me reclined in the bath, reading his scrolls of research. I did it just out of curiosity and I was quite careful with them. As I had to keep my newfound status intact, my fin was revealed... displayed at the end of the tub, in a blue-green-yellow-orange mix of hues.

I put the scroll I was reading on a table, beside the bath, and looked up. 'Hello, Nanlee.'

'I say Alec, you seemed very occupied with my work,' he replied, astounded.

'I've been going over your policies of the Aquarium and how you had bettered the standards of handling exhibitions and all. Not that it is my business anyway.'

'Mind you don't get the scrolls wet.' Nanlee was so concerned.

I showed him the table where I'd laid them. He picked them up and put them on a shelf.

He led Cynthia toward me. 'Alec, this is Cynthia. Cynthia, this is...'

'The fellow I saw in the tank,' she exclaimed. 'Wow, this is amazing. You were able to track him, then.'

'Certainly was and did, as you can see,' Nanlee smiled at her.

I nearly forgot myself for a moment as I gazed at Cynthia.

She was still cute, in a childish way, as if to be a daughter, but yet, fully grown. *Definitely would beat the old wife in the charm department.* My eyes were alit as soon as the dear girl came up close. This was not the tank with glass separating us, but someone *directly* in front of me.

'Hello,' she held out her hand. 'You have a beautiful fin.'

She bent down to stroke the extremity, which sent shivers up my spine and I became a tad aroused.

I had to play it cool, as Nanlee began to eye me with discord. 'Ahh... I had not noticed it showing... so sorry. Do pardon me.'

I tried to lower the fin underwater, but as the bath was small, I had to compromise. *But I was still aroused.*

'Now, that will do,' he said, trying to discourage the initial excitement.

"Tis alright, let her. I do not mind,' I cooed.

I continued to smile at her.

'I wish I could join you,' she drooled.

Nanlee was shocked... it was not my fault the belovèd had fallen into the lap of my attraction. (Unfortunately, during my more famous moments, I had this happen all the time... *the wife so hated it!*)

I dared her to... 'You will have to remove your dress.'

Nanlee, meanwhile, had put on a silk robe from the Far East.

It was a gift to him for his work at the Aquarium. It was multi-coloured with brown, beige and green, developing into a chinoisery-style pattern, which was quite masculine. It was soft to the touch and had a sheen to it that made the item glow. The wearer himself could not be described as less than luscious.

Cynthia took the bait (naturally) and fingered the tie at the waist. It slipped off as readily as he'd put it on... *the material could melt in one's fingers.*

Of course, Nanlee was not going to make it easy for the young lass. Underneath, it was expected otherwise... all she got was one of his finest mustard yellow linen tunics. This slightly threw tension into the room, when her aggression got the better of her and she mauled him, tearing his clothes off, nearly beating him in the process.

At last, she struck flesh and went absolutely wild on him. The kissing, stroking, and fondling began, all at once, where she dived for...

'Ahem,' I coughed aloud, sitting pretty, by myself... *wanting.*

She turned quickly to me. 'Oh, I do apologise. I did not want to make Nanlee to feel left out.'

Nanlee was hot under the collar by now and, at last, came up for air from a different kind of submergement. 'Please don't mind me. I had enough excitement for one evening. You two go on and befriend one another. I'll go off to get changed.'

He excused himself, his already ruddy cheeks redder than a sunburn.

I had to ask. 'I trust you now plan to maul me, too?'

'No,' she replied, 'Your fin is a handful as it is. But it is a lovely specimen.'

'Nothing is a handful for you, my dear.' I encouraged her to carry on her...

She looked at her too-small hands... exactly the ones that made that handprint I saw some time ago.

'Nah, I would need Nanlee's help to get you out and dry off. How long do you spend in the water?'

I had not kept track of the time. *The sands went too quickly...* 'I've been in here since... oh, before you arrived. Maybe it is time I dry off.'

She came closer to me. 'May I kiss you? You look too inviting not to and your behaviour toward me at the Circus seemed friendly enough.'

'I shall kiss thee in wet favour.' I puckered my lips and placed them on hers. She then held me at the neckline and we enjoyed one another...

...until...

Nanlee came in, better attired.

'I see you two are getting acquainted. Would you like some refreshment?'

'Ohh, rather,' I murmured. 'I would like to get out of the tub and join the air.'

'No problem.' Nanlee rushed to get a couple of towels from the cupboard and laid them on the sofa.

He and Cynthia had picked me up at each end and put me upon the towel-laden sofa. I wrapped myself, as if an Egyptian mummy, feeling snug and comforted in myself.

As my body settled into dry air, my legs reformed and I got to see my feet again. Cynthia saw the glee on my face, so she tickled my toes and I squirmed a little. Nanlee had that tunic from the Aquarium, which he'd given me to put on. *It was kind enough of him to look after it for me.*

I thanked him and draped the tunic elegantly on my body, like grace upon a god.

'I kept it for you, ol' boy,' Nanlee dismissed. 'Hungry?'

'I am, yes,' I confirmed.

He left us to scramble some titbits to nibble on, though I could see Cynthia dying for something *else*.

Her drooling continued. 'I've never been so attracted to a man like you before.'

'I believe I feel the same with you, but let us be friends for the moment and see what develops.'

I sincerely recalled the endless scrolls of affection I'd received during my career days, and I usually shrugged them off, as I was married and could not pursue the like. Now that I have become an outcast from society and the divorce had quickly finalised, there was *no way* I was going to hold back...

... but, as in all relationships, I planned to take it slow.

She put her arms around me with a loving embrace. 'You are a very exceptional being.'

'I have been through much and want to put *that* behind me.'

'I hope I can help you.'

We kissed again when Nanlee brought some foodstuffs and wine on a makeshift trolley he probably built himself for convenience.

'Here we are, grapes, nuts, bread, and wine. Help yourselves,' he motioned to the snacks.

'Thank you,' Cynthia said, as she began to nibble a slice of bread.

'Much obliged,' I replied to him, 'And I really appreciate this meeting. She is a wonderful girl, Nanlee. I would like to show her my world sometime.'

Nanlee's eyebrow furrowed. 'Beyond the land?'

'Why not?'

His eyes narrowed and I could sense a touch of envy... but it was not the kind that I was used to, which normally resulted in a row, or worse, a fight.

'Well,' he hesitated, holding back, 'We will see.'

It seemed he was a tad upset, as he thought Cynthia was his girl, although uncommitted as of yet. Naturally, he felt as if a simple plebeian.

'I can show her how we live and that there is nothing for the Mortal to fear about us. May shave off a few decades of prejudice,' I offered.

'She cannot breathe underwater,' Nanlee argued, turning to Cynthia, 'Can you?'

She shook her head.

I had to think fast. 'Neptune could accommodate her. He would be most delighted to meet her anyway, as I have already discussed her with Him.'

'Oh, would He now? You are putting the life of a lovely young woman in the hands of your mythological friend?'

The ignorance of Mortals was too much to bear and I could now understand the need for separation between them and us Mercastes. I just did not think Nanlee Q. Pymbrush would be like the *others*. I sighed deeply, nearly as upset as he was...

... *yet, I had to defend my god.* 'Neptune is more than mythology. He is life, He is our breath, He is...'

'Spare me your religious tracts,' Nanlee scorned. He turned again to Cynthia, 'Your life, my friend. Do you have as much faith as Alec here, to go underwater unaided?'

She paused, thinking about my offer. 'Could I get to know him first?'

Nanlee soothed his savagery, for her sake. 'You may. And if you may, give me a report? You could help me with my research. Find out how they live and such. I will allow that compromise.'

Cynthia pondered further, sipped a bit of wine, and agreed to do it.

I looked out the window, where the night sky emerged dominant. 'Let us discuss this further in the morning. It is getting late and Heaven knows I am tired.'

Nanlee put the food away, to be had for breakfast, and we all piled into the bedroom for a good re-set.

CHAPTER X

Morning came, arriving too deeply to awaken the most weary soul. Despite this, I awoke naked on a large sized bed, with Cynthia and Nanlee sleeping beside me. *By the sea, had we all slept together???!!* That was interesting... Nanlee looked completely entranced in a dream.

I got up from the slumbering mess around me and went to a small planked hole, nestled in the corner of the room. I relieved myself and opened the window. The sun arisen fairly, still climbing the ladder of hours, which in my opinion looked to be about the seventh or eighth rung. I returned to the bed and found that silk robe Nanlee had on the night before.

It certainly had a ring to it. I tried it on, to cover my person, as I touched its single sumptuous layer. I mused on what Cynthia would say, or do, if she saw *this* on me...

I returned to the open window and gazed at the activities done in the fair distance. I also saw my ocean home beyond the shoreline, which I sorely missed. I really wanted to take Cynthia under and firmly believed in the hospitality she would receive there.

I spun round to hear noise coming from the bed. Nanlee was stirring in his sleep, murmuring odd things. He seemed satisfied... at something. What it was, I could not reveal. *Probably not my business, anyway.*

His eyes slowly opened and a yawn emitted a haunting wave in the room. He glanced at me, with a further awareness about him.

'Morning. I can see you've borrowed my robe. It suits you,' Nanlee acknowledged, with a wink.

I looked down at the robe and agreed. 'Very fetching, but I would never want this for myself.'

'You are too humble, Alec. Your tunic was put over there, if you please,' he pointed to a makeshift dresser.

I went over and found the item. I grew fond of the tunic and thankful there was no malice between us, despite our mutual interest in Cynthia. I removed his robe and put it near his side and put on the tunic.

'There's a well in the back, if you care to freshen up,' he said.

'Nice idea, thank you.' I walked over there and took care of myself. I splashed my face and cleaned up, ready for the off.

Cynthia was still asleep and Nanlee got up and put on his robe. Once I'd finished washing up, I felt I looked my best for her.

I crept toward the bed and sat on the side.

'Morning,' I whispered in Cynthia's ear.

Life enhanced her favour when she awoke.

'Alec,' she exclaimed, giving me a hug.

'Steady, ol' thing. You are not dressed.'

'Huh?'

I lifted the covers up to show her.

'Ooops,' she cried, 'Could you hand me my dress on the side there?'

I did so and she dressed herself beneath the covers, for modesty. She needn't worry though, for if she decides to go under with me, modesty itself will have to be *discarded*.

I went over to Nanlee, who was reclaiming last night's tray. 'Going to work today?'

'Yep, I have much to do. You may come with me, or spend the time and take Cynthia into town. I would recommend a disguise.'

It had been awhile since I left the stage and wondered if anyone *would* recognise me. My profession made me a chameleon to all, so it should not be difficult to find something to segregate me from popularity.

Nanlee gave me a look. 'Had you shaved yet?'

I felt some stubble forming, which I hated, due to its scratchy feeling. I returned the look, showing it was obvious I had not.

'Well, do refrain from it. If you were clean-shaven before and people remembered you that way, then grow yourself out. Also, wear a cloak of some form. It's supposed be cooler today.'

I was surprised at his confidence. 'How do you know? Are you in touch with a god, Nanlee?'

He faced me. 'No, I am not in touch with any god. I can just feel it.'

Hmmm. 'Can I borrow one of yours?'

'Help yourself. It seems that your size is compatible with mine, if that robe has anything to state.'

Cynthia joined us, after her morning routine. She saw me and made a face. 'Eeewwhh, you look shaggy. It's not right.'

Was this disguise effective? 'Would you rather see me thrown back to the sea?'

She shook her head.

I quizzed her plainly. 'Do I look recognisable to you?'

Her reaction was more intense and she walked around me. 'It looks good enough to me. If you are able to be someone else, then do it. Wasn't that what you were paid for?'

'The actor's famed role...,' Nanlee contemplated. 'As the public had seen less of you, your costume and shaggy-face look should do. You *could* get away with it.'

'But not with me,' Cynthia teased, 'I know what to look for.'

I smiled. 'You would. Come here, you.'

I grabbed her and gave her a kiss.

'If you grew out, maybe you can blend in with society again. I could try to get used to the extra hair, I guess,' she sighed.

'I cannot work again. People will know who I was and what happened to me.'

'For a day or two, this should suffice,' Nanlee added, taking a bite of some honey-dipped bread.

I figured it would be alright for now, yet I had not planned on staying out of water like this...

... and I *itched* to return to the sea, with Cynthia in tow.

We joined Nanlee in some breakfast, which was good and nourishing. The bread was soft, the grapes had a juicy bite and the wine was sweet. I dipped my portion of bread in the wine and it tasted heavenly... nearly *mystical*, if one could call it that.

After we ate, Nanlee went off to work and Cynthia and I went separately for a walk around town. I was curious to return to the Amphitheatre to see how it was going and what plays were being performed.

The streets of Pallancium were busy, as usual. The port had ships docked from various parts of the Known World, bringing over items which will end up in private hands, markets or the theatre as costumes and/or props.

The Market was held in an alley known as Phlipadea Lane, and the area surrounding it was insanely bustling with activity. *Lucky the ships arrived in time for this.*

I had no interest in the Market, as the items there were useless to a Mercaste, (except the food, perhaps). We strolled away from the clamour to a quieter area. We walked through a residential section before I spotted the old place itself.

Ah, the haunt of the theatre, my heart raved. It was an open air set up, and anyone could come and join in to watch. Those with seats, paid and those who stood, got to take in the show for free. Paid seating was left to the more affluent, as culture was important to them, and they were as lazy as the eye can see.

Everyone was happy to contribute, even those standing who did not have a monetary burden. If there *was* money amongst that lot, they, too, threw their pennies our way. It was nice to get public support and I remembered how important my job was, as an entertainer, to ensure they got good quality showmanship. However, my style of showmanship was rather *sophisticated...* there were others that catered to the bawdier masses. It was a happy few minutes, or hours to forget oneself and one's life.

The best part was that I had not been seen as the actor, Alexander Nespor. Everyone around me saw me as an old sack. And I was satisfied with that...

... but my replacement of the moment was none other than...

... *hey, what's this?* My interest lured me to take a closer look. I held Cynthia's hand as we gathered space between the mass that lingered to watch the show, which was well underway. I felt grateful that a crowd was there and it did not impede my search for who was on stage...

... and it was none other than...

My eyes flew open...

... *it was my son, Martus Faximilus!*

No, no, it cannot be! My head ranted... he was just nearing... *how old was he?* Oh, I confess to forget. Was he *that* disciplined as to take on such a task?!! I was mesmerised to see him pick up where I'd left off. *It had not been that long, but sheeesh...*

... *it had been an eyeful to me.*

He had a speaking part, from an old play I'd performed long ago... its name eluded me now... Martus looked good on stage, *but I faired more nobler than he.* I had to ponder if he were to be thrown into the sea, mistaken for the Mercaste that was me, what would become of he?

I smiled at the prospect, as his monologue reverberated throughout the theatre, finally reaching into my hearing:

Oh Ack, ye Sun and Moon
One shall awaken thee,
To live in this dire world
Of mediocrity.
Your crown's cast awry,
Seeking shelter in Death's seeking sky.
Forever to search for ye, by-the-by,
Your thunder has been replaced, oh my!
'Tis better to be ill with shame,
Than lose face in the game.
And for your loss of fame,
I bear the blame.

The audience applauded when the monologue had finally ended. I joined in the applause, along with Cynthia. Martus took a bow and waved as he left the stage...

... a change of scene was at hand and the play continued...

... *all morning.*

Later on, Cynthia poked me at the side stating a need to eat. Time had passed and it was more profound when one spent it, watching one's progeny at the helm... *my helm.*

I looked up at the sky to see the sun nearing its midday position. I then tugged at her dress and motioned her to depart with me.

We were away from the theatre when I saw her eyes burned with inquisitiveness. 'That fellow on the stage. One minute I saw him, then next minute, I saw *you*. What was that all about?'

I smiled with pride. 'That was my son.'

'Wouldn't you like to go up and congratulate him? I am sure he'd be happy to see you. He's good, but I want to see *you* in a play.'

'I cannot go back, my love. I have been banned from society, and from family. *My son probably resents me by now… it had been too long between us.* We are fortunate we had not been discovered and I know a way to ensure no one catches our wind.'

'I'm still hungry,' she whinged.

My body's reserves were at breaking point by this time, yet, like Mercury's feet, or Apollo's sun chariot, I had to carry on. *We must move with time*, I reckoned and it will be a reckoning if we don't get on with it.

We left my son to his *own audacious career* and headed past the market for the harbour.

I pointed outward. 'You see that island there, in the distance?'

She peered carefully. 'I see it.'

'That is Clunia, where I live, when not in water.'

'It looks deserted, but for a few people,' she observed.

'Those are Mercastes, out of water. It is a place we go to dry-off. We keep in touch with our humanity. Most of them are very self-absorbed, due to their life experiences and outcasted status. They are friendly to those who get to know them better.'

'Can we go there?'

'You'll have to swim for it, for I cannot blow my cover.'

I took her to another alley, where there was easy access to the sea.

She asked, 'What about our clothes?'

'Keep them, we'll need them later.'

I looked at her.

Her breathing was fast.

'Ready?'

'I think so,' she hoped.

We dove into the sea, and as soon as I hit the water, my transformation began. I hastily removed my tunic and gave it to her.

'Wow,' Cynthia gasped, spitting water out of her mouth.

'Never mind wow, dear, get under. You'll need the Kiss from Neptune, if you are to remain underwater, beyond your normal capacity. He can oblige a visitor and friend of the Mercastes. He is also expecting to meet you.'

'So I will become a Mercaste like you?'

'Yes and no. He will offer you temporary neck-gills, which will go away when you resume your land-life. Let's go, before we get caught.'

We swam to a deeper section. Our splashing had caught the attention of a passer-by, who paid no attention.

'Mercastes are everywhere,' he frowned.

And we must be everywhere, except in the Mortal world.

CHAPTER XI

Underwater, we swam, heading for Neptune. Despite my transformation, Cynthia was still a Mortal, and a most beautiful one, at that... *but it wouldn't be long until...*

I held her hand, using all the muscle I had in my tail fin. I raced past many species and colours, waving to them, as we passed by.

'Those two are in a hurry,' one of the fish said.

His companion shrieked, 'That's a Mortal with him!'

'Oh, by Neptune, I hope they make it, or the girl will die,' an older Mercaste commented.

The sea suddenly enacted a swirling motion, not unlike the one from the Aquarium. This one, though, was different. A huge wave had formed into the kindly familiar square-like face that was Our Neptune. We finally reached the Fellow who will give my lady leave to remain with me.

'I had a feeling you would need me,' He guessed, 'I felt new blood in My realm.'

He immediately laid his hands upon Cynthia's shoulder and went for her neck. He Kissed her and gills had formed where His lips touched her.

'Now, breathe, child,' He commanded.

As she nearly lost her own air-breath, an alternative airy feeling came within her lungs. She violently exhaled. Then, she inhaled again, and it was easy, albeit a odd sensation.

'So this is what it is like to be under the sea,' she observed, fluidly.

I smiled at her and gave her my own kiss. 'Yes, my love. You are now at one with us.'

'Not exactly,' Neptune stated, 'She will require a fin, if she is to stay. I trust this arrangement is only temporary.'

'It is,' I confirmed, bowing. 'I wanted to let her see my world.'

'Is this the lady who left that handprint?'

Cynthia piped up, embarrassed at the affair, 'It was me, sir. Sorry.'

'No need to apologise,' Neptune soothed. 'You made My child very happy.'

She made a face. 'Huh?'

'Neptune refers to us as His children, from the smallest invertebrate, to the giant sperm whale and everything in between. This includes Mercastes,' I explained.

'Ah,' she nodded. 'I just find it a bit funny, that's all. I have not been called a child for years, although my companions treat me like one at times.'

'Much for their ignorance,' Neptune added. 'You know better... I know more, and Alec, here, he really cares for you, ol' girl.'

'Will I get a fin someday?'

'You must make a commitment to Alec and one to Myself,' He replied, 'You are most welcome here and I would be proud to add you to My realm. Yet, I think you have another interest. I can see it in your face.'

She blushed, thinking about Nanlee.

The blush had not gone un-noticed by Him. 'I do have a friend, who is sort of more than that, but we are uncommitted as of yet,' she admitted.

'If you want a tail fin, you will have to submit to the water,' He stated.

She looked at me and I replied to her, 'No need to answer now. This is just for you to see this world for yourself.'

'I know. I do not want to commit yet, but I will have to contemplate on this,' she said.

Neptune was most inviting. 'No rush. No pressure. Just enjoy yourself with Alec.'

'I'm taking the girl to Clunia, to see how Mercastes live on land.'

'Good for you. You both go and savour the moment. No sense hanging about with an old codger like Me, eh?' Neptune let a laugh escape.

'Actually, I am more comfortable down here and loving it,' Cynthia beamed, 'This is a truly unique experience a human could ever encounter. Thank you for having me.'

'You are most welcome,' Neptune smiled, 'My prayers and love are with you. Fare thee well.'

He then towered over us to carry on His duty of care to fish-kind.

We continued our merry swim and led her further into the deep. I showed her some of my favourite discoveries and even went to that old shipwreck I discovered some time ago.

'And now, to Clunia.' I led her further toward the inviting shore that awaited us.

After a few moments, we reached the sandy shore, with some rocks thrown in for good measure. She helped me roll out of the water and climbed the bank. As she still had our clothes from before, she threw me the tunic and I laid it on my fin. The sun was now baking hot (after early morning coolness), so I used the opportunity to sun myself. Cynthia put on her dress for modesty, though the people around her walked around naturally. She scanned the area and found other Mercastes hanging about, chatting, drying off from their swim, and making love.

She asked, 'Is it always like this?'

I giggled a bit, as I saw the love makers getting more passionate. 'Yes it is; relaxing and very easy-going. No Mortal judgement or rules upon us, which makes it all the more appealing for those who wish to get away and those *forced* to.'

'Gosh,' she said, still watching everything around her. She laid down, relaxing, nearly dozing in the sand. My legs were finally formed and I put on the tunic she threw at me. We spent awhile just feeling love and pleasure within. The sky was perfect, but for the sizzling sun upon us. Some of the Mercastes who ventured away from the sea made the decision to return and hastily jumped in. It was exhilarating to feel the cool sea around one as the impact is made.

I had a desire for a meal. 'Hungry?'

'Is that the time? I'd forgotten all about it, yes,' she exclaimed.

'There's a cove nearby, teeming with many fish, usually the smaller ones.'

She made a face. 'Live fish?'

Her hesitant stance was getting annoying to me. *Was she that naive?* 'What do you think?'

'Ummm.....ugh,' she frowned.

'They are just small nibble-fry types, nothing nasty about them. I am certain you have eaten fish before?'

'I have, but not live.'

Ah... so that's it. 'I confess a sly trend toward cooking. We could build a fire and I can cook the meal, if you go out to gather. Fair deal?'

'Shame it will not come with anything else.'

'We rough it on Clunia. Do remember we *are* fish and normally live in the sea. This is a place where one could catch the breath, as it were.'

I led her to the cove, which had a cave entrance where a bucket lay still. Rock pools formed nearby, where many of the tiddlers took shelter or swam away, if they did not like it. Anything massive would not get out so easily and made fine catches for multiples of Mercastes awaiting a feast.

Cynthia then looked at me and went all moral. 'If your people are fish and you eat fish, isn't that cannibalism?'

'We are part of a life chain. Fish eat other fish. Mercastes are an exception, unless they provoke the likes of a whale or a shark.'

'So you've no conscience regarding these matters?'

I, meanwhile, had *attempted* to start a fire, using some old sticks lying about from a hedgerow. Frustration set in, although not her fault, and my temper was at a lesser ebb than normal. I threw the stick away and turned to her, glaring...

... *and unfortunately, I snapped.* 'Would you rather see me starve?'

'Forgive me if I made you mad. By Jove, I was just curious... please. I'm sorry,' she begged.

I let go of another stick. 'No, 'tis nay your fault. It is me who should apologise. I take the blame.' I kissed her to reassure her all was fine with me... *though I would not consider myself fine at the moment.*

She ripped a piece of fabric off her now-dry dress. 'Would this help?'

I took the cloth and tried again, rubbing the sticks. Another Mercaste, seeing what I was *still* attempting to do, found a small parchment he saw lying about.

'Try this,' he said.

I thanked him and put the item in with the stick pile and continued rubbing. Soon, the hoped-for blaze emerged, *but for how long?*

'Could you please get us some fish, dear? There is a bucket at the cave for you to gather them,' I told Cynthia.

'Just return it when you're finished,' the other Mercaste added.

'Alright.' Cynthia went off to retrieve the bucket and catch some fish.

The Mercaste followed to help her, noting her *Mortal* tendencies. They brought back some tiddlers; hardly enough to fill one's mouth with. The Mercaste took the bucket from her and handed it to me. I took a fish out of the bucket and impaled it upon a stick and put it over the fire. I did the same to the rest, then I wanted to test the young lass.

'Let's see you go fish on your own, love,' I ordered.

She did so, whilst the Mercaste remained with me. She went to a different rock pool and mimicked what she'd seen my compatriot did. When she returned, there was quite a lot of fish and a large crab.

'Wow, nice haul, kid,' I complemented her.

The crab looked at me, pleading silently, knowing its fate.

'Please don't eat me. I had been stuck in that damn pool for many hours and I need to return to the open waters. I've got a wife and multiple children. May you please send me back,' it requested.

I felt bad for the little guy and Cynthia's earlier argument and Mortal tendencies denied us a more luxurious dish.

After muttering many a cuss under the breath, I took the crab and tossed it into an area which led to the main body of water.

'Much obliged, sir,' the crab said, floating away. I had wondered if this happened to me, *would the other person be as merciful?*

I went back to the fire, where the Mercaste and Cynthia was cooking the fish that was successfully collected for food. Thankfully, the many fish that was gathered made up for the loss of that lovely crab. *It was just as well...*

... we were full anyway and death's door would have been vain for that crab. I was full, Cynthia was full and the other Mercaste had strolled away, after having his fill. He took the bucket back to that cave entrance, as a favour and kindness, for the next person to help himself.

Once we'd finished eating, I put out the fire and chucked the bones. I held Cynthia close and gave her a kiss. We began to fumble about somewhat, *and it was rather fun.*

However, a lone figure emerged and I recognised him as Colpert, the fellow I met on a previous occasion. As he approached us, I saw that his face was grim with concern.

'Hello,' I waved.

'Good that I caught you,' Colpert said, 'Your friend Nanlee has been taken and dumped into the tank. He must have been mistaken for you...'

CHAPTER XII

It took some time to recover from the news. I rubbed my head and thought... *how could they have mistaken Nanlee for myself?* My hand went to my now fuzzy chin and my disguise was working a treat...

... and noted by Colpert.

'You're growing out, I see,' he said, 'You've sported a more shadowy look,' he pointed at my chin.

I felt the razor sharp stubble elongating nicely. It had made an excellent concealment, but at a price I had not expected.

'That I am. It was the only way for me to get the girl away from the Mortal world without recognition. Do you know what happened to Nanlee?'

He contemplated the events in his mind. He then noticed Cynthia.

'Hello,' he said to her, 'I'm Colpert, and you?'

Cynthia got up to meet him, offering her hand. 'Cynthia Tarquinne. How do you do?'

'Mercaste or Mortal?'

She looked back at me. 'Mortal, with a temporary neck-gill. I had not received my fin yet; I am uncommitted.'

Colpert had a sly face upon the last bit of her sentence. 'Uncommitted?'

'Yes, I had not decided if I should leave the Mortal world or not. I feel that I am fine as I am.'

'Well, my dear,' he went on, 'You may find that life below the sea is far better than life atop.'

She did not think of his comment when I barged in, asking again, 'So what happened to Nanlee?'

'From the message I received, he went to work that day. His superior, being slightly drunk the previous night, saw him and thought he was you.'

'Looks like I have another date with Neptune,' I sighed. 'Cynthia, I am sorry to cut your visit to Clunia short, but we have work to do.'

She got up, brushing the sand off her dress. 'If Nanlee is now underwater, would he have received the Kiss and fin by now?'

I took her aside. 'He would, yes. Neptune does not ever let a Mortal die without due cause. If a Mortal accidentally falls into His realm, and he could swim away, then no matter; if he cannot, then Neptune will help him. In Nanlee's case, however, the Great Sea Lord would definitely intervene. He knows of Nanlee, from a previous conversation, so I am certain that he is safe, probably putting on a show at the Circus.'

Cynthia remarked, 'For all that research he does, this really takes the cake! What time is it anyway?'

I smiled and looked up at the sun, which was gaining its westerly foothold through the hours. 'Nearly the fourth or fifth hour, post-meridian. The tanks will be cleaned soon and the day's fish will be swirling into our water.'

* * * * * *

Meanwhile, Nanlee was still in the tank. His clothes were removed and he gained what he needed to survive in the tank. *Neptune saw to that.* Yet, he found the experience invigorating, considering *this* was what he spent much of his life studying. Reading about fish was one thing; *being a fish...* well... that was an entirely different life altogether. Nanlee kept the pretence of his Mercaste state and tried to satisfy the crowd watching him.

He reflected on what happened to him. The day seemed to beget favour, to his knowledge and it did not seem unusual in any way. Nanlee swam about, intensely going over of the events to try to get to the bottom of why *he* was sunk to the bottom of the sea. On the way to work, Nanlee walked past a thorny hedge, with some of its branches sticking outward... ready to strike at the unknown. To his misfortune, he had an entanglement with the unruly branch and it struck his neck area, leaving a bloody scratch mark.

As Nanlee had his pride, he disregarded the incident and moved on...

... still bleeding from the hedge wound.

Upon entering the Aquarium, he passed by some staff and workmen, as well as his superior Raybin. Raybin hurriedly walked past, muttering nonsense to himself; a result of rather loud night in town. Nanlee pressed on, ignoring that too...

...until...

Raybin had a sudden turnabout. Remembering the incident regarding the freeing of a Mercaste on site, he stormed forth and headed for Nanlee...

... raving, 'What are you doing out of the tank??'

'I beg your pardon, sir,' Nanlee responded, most confused at his question.

'You... I saw you the other day... *that Mercaste...*,' Raybin's eyes widened and he spotted the cut on Nanlee's neckline. 'You're... you're the fellow!'

Nanlee was very disturbed by this. 'If you must know, I had an argument with a bramble hedge, alright?'

The stupor took full effect on Raybin, who was *determined* to win this spat with Nanlee. 'You get back into the tank, before I...'

Nanlee challenged him, arms crossed. 'Before you what?'

A few agonising minutes went by. The two men pressed eyes together.

'Get the hell back into the tank, or I will have you sent away for experimental dissection,' he threatened, *in delirium.*

'Excuse me,' Nanlee further challenged, 'Do you know who I am?'

'YOU'RE THAT MERCASTE!'

'I am not a Mercaste, I am Nanlee Q. Pymbrush, Chief Research Scientist.'

Raybin sneered viciously, 'By Jove you are.' He left and commanded to the workmen to secure Nanlee for the tank.

The workers held Nanlee into a grip, stripping him to bare flesh and threw him into the water. Raybin had stepped over the mark *this* time.

Nanlee was rather embarrassed at such actions against him and dived further below for cover, using the cardboard scenic dioramas to hide.

A baritone voice swelled throughout the waters, calling, 'Nanlee Quimsey Pymbrush.'

Nanlee responded by looking around him, with panic in his mind. It did not do him any good, for he only confronted a kindly face, which formed from the bubbly actions. There was no need to fear after all... *but when one faces a god*, then... it could make for keen discourse.

'My son, you are safe. Yes, I do know your full name, but that can be between us, if you wish. Let me Kiss you and we shall speak,' the voice kindly said.

An air capacity formed suddenly on Nanlee's neck and a fin began to emerge below his lower region. The earlier cut had healed in the salty waters, caressed with Neptune's love. The surprise that was felt was priceless and Nanlee took to swimming like a fish with ease. There was a sense of calmness about him and he felt a small sensation on his neck, where the gill was, which allowed him to breathe.

Nanlee looked up at Neptune with intense awe. 'I do not know how to thank you. I could have died down here. I was taken by surprise by my superior, who thought I was Alec.'

'That superior of yours, I reckon, is a clouded man and a very troubled one, indeed. Alec had told me about you. You're the one who works at that Aquarium and is a friend of Cynthia's, I believe.'

'Yes, Sir, that I am,' he affirmed.

'It is good to have met you all, and, as you will be within My realm for awhile, you are a welcome guest,' Neptune assured.

'When will I return to the landed world? I have a job; I have work to do.'

'You will not be going anywhere. If I am not mistaken, your superior has threatened to dissect you, when you last had words with him in your normal capacity. I recommend you remain here with us, for now. I can pass a message to Alec to take over for you until this foggy mess has cleared up.'

Nanlee was astonished. 'Alec knows nothing about being a research scientist! He is a bloomin' actor, for Jove sake!'

'So,' Neptune continued, 'As an actor, he must fulfil a role, does he not? Let him do your bit, and we will get there in the end. You will be restored shortly.'

Nanlee shrugged, 'So I just swim around all day and play contentment?'

'Aye,' voiced The answer. 'Please do not worry. I will take care of you.'

Nanlee smiled and swam away, still entrapped within the watery boundaries of the Circus.

CHAPTER XIII

I returned to the sea, having received the message from Neptune that I would deputise for Nanlee at the Aquarium, whilst he was indisposed. The beard would have to remain and I could be just plain *Mr Nespor*. I trusted that the staff there would accept me until I figure out a way to clear up the mess regarding Nanlee. It was most unfortunate, inconvenient... *and they were unaware of the scheme.*

After spending the night undersea, Cynthia and I had gone to her place to introduce me to the Threescore. It would also serve to explain her recent whereabouts to them, as she thought they would be worried about her.

On the way, we discussed a way she could remain with me, for the time being.

'How would you like to be my assistant? We could work together and plan a rescue for Nanlee,' I suggested.

She was ecstatic. 'Oh yes, please. That would be great, but it is temporary?'

'It would be, yes… but our friendship will remain.'

We held hands, then she said, 'I'd like that very much. It will be a good way to keep his job afloat meanwhile.'

I put my hand to my head and groaned at the nautical pun she made.

'I am not that bad with mirth,' she defended.

'Still corny, babe.'

We reached her home. I felt sore about meeting other Mortals, especially if there was a chance of recognition. *Yet, it was inevitable.*

She asked, 'Ready?'

'I think it would do them good to know who it is taking care of you,' I exhaled.

Our knock was soon answered by a stout fellow, balding and of mature years… Nay-Smith.

A voice called out from within. 'Cynthia, where have you been?'

'I've been with this fellow, Alexander Nespor,' Cynthia announced, walking in and showing me to her companions.

Buckingham stood up. 'The actor turned Mercaste?'

She blushed. 'Yes.'

'He is hardly what I remember him as,' Cateliffe remarked, peering at me.

'Looks nothing like him,' Nay-Smith added.

I touched the beard, which was doing a good job of it. 'It is me. I grew my own to be able to escape the last licks of fame. I was at the theatre sometime earlier, and it is apparent that I have been *forgotten* after my son took over.'

'What did I tell you, eh,' Buckingham interjected smugly. 'I knew that would happen.'

'Yes, and he is *damn good* at it, too,' I replied, with a touch of jealousy, but there was more to tell. 'There has been an incident at the Aquarium and Nanlee was thrown in the tank.'

Cateliffe couldn't believe it. 'Why?'

'They thought he was me. We do look alike somewhat, save the beard,' I replied.

Buckingham retorted, 'I think he'll keep himself buoyant for while.'

More puns... augh!

'So you've been looking after our girl, then,' Nay-Smith charged in.

I faced them. 'She has been fine with me and I will take her on as my assistant, to help with Mr Pymbrush's research work.'

'That should keep you both out of trouble,' Buckingham quipped. 'Does Raybin know of this arrangement?'

My mind played on... *I had not thought that far.* 'Not to my knowledge. If he is that poorly in knowing his own staff, then I think we will fill the space nicely.'

'Good,' Cateliffe felt less anxious. 'I hope you know what his job entails.'

'I have read some of his work already. I stayed at his flat for a bit and I read some of his scrolls to pass the time.'

Nay-Smith asked, 'Are you planning a rescue?'

'We will plan for one, yes,' I paused. 'You really found it hard to recognise me?'

The three men conferred amongst themselves. 'Your beard threw us off. We're used to you without it. Most others are too,' Buckingham replied.

'We thought you were an average fellow. No one special,' Cateliffe observed.

'I am most pleased to hear that, so I can be just plain old Mr Nespor.'

It seemed I was too hopeful in my optimism, but if one did not have faith in *something*, the cause will surely fail.

Buckingham offered us some wine and I motioned Cynthia to come over.

Cateliffe teased, 'Is Cynthia your new girl?'

I took no notice of the silliness. 'She is a friend and the one I wanted to meet at the Aquarium.'

'So it was *you* who created all the fuss with her,' Nay-Smith realised.

'Aye, it was me. And what of it,' I challenged them.

'We knew she was keen on a Mercaste, but we did not think we would meet you. I confess we created a bit of fuss over this matter too. We're sorry,' Buckingham apologised.

I suddenly felt groggy and noticed I'd been out of water for some time. 'Do you have a bath?

Nay-Smith was astounded. 'What do you need a bath for?'

'I have to submerge myself once a day. It's a Mercaste thing. No need to be ashamed.'

Buckingham joked. 'Don't leave a fishy smell behind.'

I rolled my eyes. 'Mercastes are cleaner and have no real fish smell because they are an acquired species, not to-the-sea-born.'

'As if there's a difference,' Cateliffe scoffed.

'A fish is a fish,' Nay-Smith agreed.

'Not quite. This is where Mortals get it wrong. Every fish is different and we are all loved and cared for by the same Master.'

The Threescore all sported cynical faces in unison. 'Who?'

'Why, Neptune, of course,' I beamed proudly.

Cateliffe's bubble burst. 'Well that makes sense, then. The bath is upstairs. You will have to grab the bucket over there, and go to the well outside. Let me show you.'

He led me up a small flight of stairs and the bath was round the corner. I also saw the relief spot, which was handy all the same. It was a cubicle of a room, done in white, comparable to Nanlee's.

'Have Cynthia fill your bath. After all, she's now *your* assistant,' Cateliffe smirked, as he left me.

I would not have her like *that*, but he was correct. I then told Cynthia to help fill the bath, which I had a feeling she would hate me for, but...

... it would be a way to define, if her love for me was solid.

'I agreed to be your working assistant, not a domestic slave,' she grumbled.

I led her toward a different path, with a sly temptation to reel her in. 'You can join me, if y'want.'

She squirmed a bit in thought when she conceded to my request and offer.

I handed her the bucket.

She went to the well outside to fill it and repeated the task several times, up and down, until the tub was at a reasonable level.

She was about to go up to join me, when Nay-Smith called, 'You're not going up there with him?!'

'What of it? I filled the bath for Alec and he said I could join him.'

'It may be a squeeze for you both,' Buckingham chimed in. 'I hope you are willing to embark on such an experience.'

'Don't do anything I wouldn't do,' Cateliffe warned.

Buckingham interrupted, 'He'll turn into a fish, and one cannot do anything with a fish.'

'Except eat it,' Nay-Smith finished the sentence, laughing.

Cynthia was not offset by their silly, sometimes austere and very boyish attitudes. She stomped upstairs, where she joined me in the bath water. My fin was taking up much of the room, but as she is a small woman, I found room for her.

We had a wonderful time together in the bath and my fin was lovingly stroked. I was becoming more fond of her by the moment, and not just due to a fin massage.

As the beard was preventing my notice to the public, I decided to keep it for now. However, my true image would be something to die for, *on a latter day*.

'You sure you do not mind this,' I pointed to the beard.

She made a face. 'How long will you keep it for?'

How long... how long is a piece of silk... how long was a fish from nose to tail? I tried answer this. 'Until the matter with Nanlee is cleared. We're to go to the Aquarium and you will need to be with me.'

'Will you stay here or at Nanlee's?'

'I must return there, as I need to catch up with what he's researching. It will also keep those companions of yours at bay, and prevent further inquisitiveness on their part.'

'That's understandable.'

'They're lively for late middle-aged men, aren't they?'

She made another face. 'They're alright, when they are not flirtatious.'

'I cannot imagine that, but I accept it. They do care for you, though, that is very apparent. Yet, they are men, and *men are men*... but *I* can marry you, they cannot.'

'Why not?

Now I made a face. 'Would you?'

She paused. 'Erm... nah. Cateliffe tried it on with me once.'

'Did he now? What did you say?'

'Another time, perhaps, or something like that. He still pines to have me.'

I laughed heartily and the water splashed over the side. 'They are good folk, but I would not want to date them either.'

She smiled and we spent a few more moments before we decided to dry-off. Cynthia climbed out and got a towel around her. I remained helpless.

'Oh, I'm so sorry,' she said. 'Do you need help?'

Duhhhh, my love.

'I'll get Cateliffe. He seems game and this will serve him right for teasing me.'

She scampered out and went into another room to get dressed, before bringing Cateliffe to do the honours.

'You're a heavy sort,' he whinged. 'Just about to fill a course for about a hundred guests.'

Enough of the jokes, man! 'At least I'd be the tastiest dish at the party,' I intoned, dryly.

Cateliffe appreciated the quirk of fishy humour, whereupon he gave me a towel, after laying me down on the floor. He left the room to give me privacy.

'Serves him right out,' Cynthia sneered.

'Off the plate,' I sniggered.

'I'll get your clothes for you.'

'Much obliged.'

We dressed and had a small meal, prior to our departure to Nanlee's place. Once we reached his flat, it was not locked, so we let ourselves in. All was left undisturbed, since our last visit. I then went through the research scrolls again and wondered how Nanlee was taking to his newfound status as a Mercaste, if only for a short spell.

CHAPTER XIV

Nanlee remained within the Circus until the time when they cleared out the tank for cleaning. He got caught up in the swirl, like everybody else, and cast away into the open sea. He went with the flow, and felt the intense rush like a flume. It felt disorienting and slightly unnerving; he had to admit it was *exciting*, nevertheless.

Once at sea, he explored his surroundings... even finding that sunken misery I spotted some time ago. He was easily breathing through the gills and taking it all in. He dipped into the opening, where he found a strange girl. She was sitting alone, looking out at what was once a porthole. Her countenance displayed a hint of sadness and Nanlee was unsure to approach. Being an overall friendly fellow, and eager to help, he approached her carefully.

'Hello, young maid, I'm Nanlee Q. Pymbrush.'

She gazed at him, very surprised he *bothered* to take an interest.

'My name's Aphrothia,' she answered sullenly.

He came closer. 'That is a lovely name, my girl. Are you alright? You seem preoccupied. Do tell me what happened to you.'

She turned to him and the melancholy took hold. 'My family and I had a difference of opinion and they expelled me. They could not cope with me and I chose the way of the Mercaste.'

'What did you disagree on?'

'Which god was best. They have their opinion, I have mine. They obviously did not agree and felt their way was better and far more sociable. *I do not see faith as a social animal.* It is as personal as going to one's toilet. I left them and decided to make my way here. It is the only way for me.'

'So there's no one there for you,' Nanlee surmised.

'No. I hate them and desire to dwell no further on the matter.'

Nanlee remembered the little island of Clunia. 'I can take you to a nice place where no one cares what one believes in, and where we can be alone under the stars.'

'That sounds too good to be true and anyway, it looks like rain,' came the desolate reply.

'Don't be like that. Maybe I can help you sheer off that gloom. Let's go.'

He encouraged the lass out of the hiding place and they swam to the promised shore of Clunia, where they took refuge and solace in one another.

'I was sent here by mistake,' Nanlee confessed.

Aphrothia recovered slightly to ask, 'What did they do to you?'

'I was mistaken for a real Mercaste by my superior at work. He was not quite right when he came into the office after a night out and, in a most unsuitable state of mind, he had me thrown into the tank. Thus, I am now here. There is a real Mercaste that's a spitting image of me, with variation and a slight age difference. You know, you look like someone I know, too.'

She laughed, showing the self that Nanlee waited for. 'There is no one in *this* place that could look like me.'

'Ah, but there is,' he insisted. 'And I see I have broken through your sadness.'

She looked about. 'I see you have,' she smiled.

He beamed in return. 'Now that's better. We can snuggle here and watch the stars.'

'What did you do before you were thrown in the tank?'

'I did research for the Aquarium, dealing with exhibitions, and fish life, well being and all that.'

Realisation pierced sharply in her mind. 'You mean that dreaded Circus?'

'Oh, I do not think it is that dreadful, my dear,' Nanlee dismissed.

'I would never ever want to be put on display, or worse. There is no reason to, and for others to gawp at *our anguish*.'

He hesitated. 'I guess you're right. You never know these things unless you've been through it yourself.'

'So you were forced to leave?'

'Stripped bare and thrown in, I'm afraid.'

'How ghastly! You should go after them,' she suggested.

Nanlee was due for a sort of measure for the inconvenience. 'I think not. Besides, I confess I am enjoying *this* existence more. It rubs off on you and it can be gotten used to.'

'It is lovely, though lonely,' she reflected. 'If I were to return, there would be no where to go.'

'If I returned, I would go to my flat and search for vacancies elsewhere.'

'So you would take up the Mortal mantle again?'

'I think so,' he said, 'And perhaps take you with me. Heaven knows I would never return to the Aquarium. I have a feeling there is something going on.'

'You're a brave soul, sir.'

'It's Nanlee, pet.'

They hugged. A spark of captivation set off between them.

'I know this will seem too forward of me to say, but I find you very attractive,' Aphrothia stated.

He grinned. 'I find you a suitable Mortal dish.'

'But I am no longer Mortal.'

'Takes one to eat one.' He pressed his nose into her side and nuzzled. She held him close and found him more delightful. They began to kiss and fondle one another. A quick glance around the immediate area revealed many Mercaste couples who indulged in expressive lovemaking.

'By the way, what does the Q stand for in your name?'

He giggled, not really giving much thought to her question. 'Quimsey, my love.'

She laughed, 'It truly suits you.'

Nanlee and Aphrothia remained on the beach and soon they were asleep in each other's arms under the starry night.

* * * * * *

I went to Nanlee's office with Cynthia the following morning. Paper scrolls piled on the desk and I decided to go to the Circus to supervise the preparation of today's exhibition. We went to the tank to see it ready for the new batch of fish and Mercastes. Everything seemed fine, so I let the labourers get on with their work and I returned to the office.

Cynthia enquired, 'So what's the plan for Nanlee?'

'Depends if he gets caught up in the vacuum,' I dryly answered.

'It looks as if you've been thrown in at the deep end.'

That's a right cheek if ever there was one. 'Put an end to it, yea?' I ruffled through the desk and found that bottle of wine Nanlee and I shared previously. I also found my favourite vintage, unopened. 'Get the gobs out, my girl. There's a '69 available.'

Cynthia found the goblets and we took in some mighty nice wine, but not a lot, *as we were working*.

She put the cup down, when a burbling sound occurred within. A voice called out and I instinctively spat out the bit of wine I hadn't swallowed. It took me aback, yet I had a sneaky feeling I knew who it was.

'Neptune?'

The voice went sarcastic. 'Who did you expect, Bacchus?'

'Well...,' I waited.

'Well anyway, Bacchus is having a party and I am here in his stead,' Neptune replied. 'Damn fool didn't invite me anyway. Never does.'

I went all sarcastic too. 'I wonder why.'

'Enough! I have a message for you. Nanlee's safe and in deep water. At the moment he's spending time with a lady Mercaste on the island of Clunia. He's in fair company and happy, though that girl's a handful.'

Cynthia folded her arms in slight envy. Neptune noted this. 'I thought you were keen on Alec, my dear. Are you?'

'I am,' she answered, 'Nanlee is a good sort, slightly predictable, never boring though. I miss him, yet, Alec here is quite remarkable.'

'Taken with him, are you? Nanlee has been a good friend to you. Alec can be more and desires it so,' the god revealed.

She looked at me, and I held her, saying, 'I do want you for me. I grow fond of you more each day I spend with you. If ever this nonsense clears up, I plan to move on, but with you.'

'That is sweet,' she kissed me, then peered at the goblet. 'I find it funny that a god could communicate through a wine vessel, sending messages and such. Next thing you know, they'll be sending voice communications through the walls.'

Then, she laughed at her own silly comment.

I spoke into my vessel. 'Anything else?'

'Um... not really, though you might wish to keep an eye on that paperwork that's littering the desk next to you. I think you will be interested in one of the items there. Keep an eye on that superior who dislodged Nanlee, too. I do not care for such a man. I am glad you are doing well in the Mortal world, but see that no one sees you speaking into a wine cup. It may look suspicious.'

The voice then dimmed and the drink bubbled before going still, becoming drinkable again. I took a large sip of it, finishing the lot, before the gods took over again. Cynthia's was full to some lesser level and laughter was heard throughout the room. She leapt about, nearly spilling the contents out of surprise.

'I did not think the gods were that mischievous,' Cynthia yelped.

'They can be, if in the mood. I thought I knew Neptune, but alas, I have not yet plunged beneath His surface,' I commented, *with my own nautical pun.*

We sat there and fiddled into the papers to find the keen bit that Neptune was on about. So far, there was nothing enticing and no serious projects to undergo...

... but wait, I did find something that triggered a sensor or two.

A slip of paper crossed my sight and I picked it up. It was a bill to Tarquinne Fisheries for a serious amount, yet to be posted.

I showed Cynthia the paper. 'Do you know about this?'

She shrugged. 'No, I do not. Just because my father was involved in the business does not make *me* privy to it.'

'Well, I wonder.' I put the paper back and had a good think. 'You don't suppose the Aquarium is selling some fish on the side to the factories to be...'

'... made up as food,' she finished my sentence. 'You could be endangered, you know.'

'We all can be, even Nanlee and that tart he's with.'

'How do you know she's a tart?'

'Have you seen a mermaid? Come on, as alluring as they are, they do not come otherwise. That is the appeal of the ocean. All that salt preserves the beauty and wow... you've made it... that is, IF you survive and take on the Kiss.'

Cynthia got insecure. 'Am I just as inviting to you?'

I got up from the bureaucratic mess of a desk. 'Your plainness makes you simple. Sometimes simple is more than enough, but we mustn't judge the girl. Every Mercaste has a story, male and female alike, and most of them are rather tragic, one way or t'other. Please do not feel out of sorts about it, because my dear, you are *my* sort and, as I've said earlier, I do want you for myself.'

'Good gods, you will have me!' She jumped into my arms and kissed me, despite the ever growing fuzzy facial presence...

... which in the god's name I am dying to shave off!!

Cynthia went pensive. 'I recall the Threescore made some lewd fish jokes at us. I am beginning to wonder about that.'

'Yea, me too,' I strained to think of it. 'We've got to get to Nanlee before...'

'Steady on,' she halted me, 'We're to stay for the job, yes?'

I did remember that and did not care a fig for Nanlee's employment. Fish welfare, my fin! *They were eating us alive!*

I went to confront that superior, who threw *me* in the tank afore. *What was his name... Raybin?* I thought better of it, but I had to clear this nonsense up; I planned to go for the real matter of the fisheries. I took Cynthia to Raybin's office, where the secretary pointed the way toward the Circus, where he was supervising the latest catches...

... and I remained calm and unimpressed.

I saw the blighter standing by the tank, watching the fish go by. The fish's reflections told me enough and gave me further cause to see this dreggy Mortal.

CHAPTER XV

The fellow looked like a leech in my eyes... feeding off the money and blood of others...

... and not necessarily for healing purposes, in the case of the latter.

I took the plunge. 'Mr Raybin?'

He spun around, his once-combed hair flipping over to one side, giving me a grin of gapped teeth. 'Take a look at all these rare specimens we've here today. Aren't they just lovely?'

A rhetorical question needed no answer.

'They are splendid; a fine lot,' I uttered with contempt.

I was grateful he did not recognise me, as yet. I stood there, glaring at him.

'Was there something I could help you with?'

I went for the throat. 'How much of these fish get returned to the sea? Are any saved for, umm... shall we say, *alternative* uses?'

A bitter pause awaited. Raybin composed himself and smiled nervously. 'You're not a reporter or auditor?'

I so wished I could take this to another level, but without the embroilment (which could char me for life). 'No, I am just a curious spectator. I attend these exhibitions regularly and I have heard a Mr Pymbrush being responsible for the welfare of these specimens.'

'He does, sir,' Raybin squirmed a bit, 'But he has disappeared somehow...'

What a trail-off!

I cleared my throat. 'Word has it that you had him thrown into the tank the other day, which had jettisoned that day's finest. You do not happen to have located him by now, eh?'

'Jettisoned the finest?' Raybin's anxiety went off-the-scale. 'I...I.., I cannot know what happened to...' He went to the tank looking around frantically at all the Mercastes present, who, in their inconspicuous way, had tried to dodge his lecherous (*to them*) glancing by hiding at the rear of the tank.

I said a quick prayer before shouting, 'You cast him out into the sea, didn't you, you fucking Mortal lout!'

'Oh, *I* did that?' He paused, muttering aimlessly to himself, 'I'm so sorry... so sorry.'

I then made a reference to that item I found on Nanlee's desk. 'And what about the invoice to Tarquinne Fisheries?'

Raybin glared daggers at me. 'How do you know of this?'

'As I am deputising for Nanlee, I saw the bill regarding the same.'

The man was cornered... I saw it in his eyes; as for his face... well, he made a failed attempt to keep it. 'You have some gall coming here, unauthorised, assuming someone's employment and going through private affairs of my staff.'

'If it was part of the job, it cannot be private. I was put in charge by Neptune Himself, as your Aquarium deals with His charges.'

Mythology flew in the face of business and smacked it one, good and proper.

'N--N--Neptune,' he stuttered, realising the importance of the name. 'I ought to bring you on charges, you know, you...,' Raybin looked at me, and the realisation came. 'You are not Pymbrush, you are an impostor!'

'I am a personal friend of his and it was something he would have approved of, had a decision been made... for the spell... however, you put things in chaos and I, as his friend, must set it right. Now, tell me what you do with these fish after hours.'

My insistence paid off. Although he remained angry with me, I could not help the redress.

He then began to talk. 'We retain a few fish for the factories to tin-up to sell to the public. We receive a share from that toward the purposes of the Aquarium.'

'And your own purses, I gather,' I smiled, knowingly. 'A tin-up? That will be one for Neptune to ponder.'

Raybin's countenance changed dramatically as soon as I pushed My Lord upon him. 'You won't spread this, yeah? I've a reputation to think of.'

'Yea, and your purse-strings. Recover Pymbrush and maybe I will forget this little chat we've had.'

The stuttering continued. 'Y--y--yes, yes, recover Pymbrush. But how? I do not know where the guy is, dammit!'

His frustration was fetching to watch.

'I could be of assistance, if I may,' I kindly offered.

Raybin tugged at my tunic. 'Please find him. You seem to know more than I.'

'So you will stop the sinister plots against Neptune's Own?'

'Yes, yes, I will contact the factory and break the contract.'

'Good.' I saw him quiver and tempted to break it to him...

... which I did, ceremoniously.

'You do not remember me, do you?'

He gazed hard. 'No, I do not think so.'

'A while back, there was a Mercaste released from the tank that you forced Pymbrush to return.'

'Umm...,' he thought hard. 'I do recall something like that happening. Yes.'

Tenterhooks, anyone? 'I… was that Mercaste.'

I left it at that and walked away. Raybin bolted into my direction, stopping in my tracks, and begging in desperation. 'Can you get Pymbrush?'

'Cease the treatment you're causing the fish as well as your nocturnal excursions, which are affecting your day-time judgement.'

'How dare you tell me what I do in my personal time?!'

'How dare you cast an innocent abroad, sir,' I shouted back.

I turned on my heel and left the dimwit to his moral squalor, to find Cynthia waiting in the corridor.

'I had him. I had him eating out of a fin,' I grinned.

'Neptune will be pleased,' Cynthia said.

'Not if He knows what these bastards are doing to His children.'

Cynthia and I walked into the office to collect a few bits, and left the Aquarium to look for Nanlee.

And I had a pretty good idea where he was.

We walked toward the shoreline again and removed our outerwear. After diving into the sea, the transformation began on me. Cynthia just was able to breathe underwater.

She cried, 'Why can't I get a fin?'

'Oh, whinge, you must commit yourself, remember? Have you made that decision yet?'

She slowly swam away, into the sea for a think. She returned, saying, 'No I had not. Events took their turn.'

'And so it seems to be,' I nodded, 'I understand.'

I held her hand as we swam toward Clunia.

It wasn't too far, and as I saw the sandy shore, I prepared to roll upon it, whilst Cynthia just climbed out, still without her fin. I let out a sigh, wishing she would commit to me and put her Mortal status aside.

I glanced around, greeted to a shore of endless lovemaking on all sides. Some paused to wave hello at me. Guessing why we were here, (for news spreads on lonely islands quickly), one of them pointed to an alcove, where Nanlee and that girl was.

'Thank you,' I called out, as Cynthia was still drying me off.

The Mercaste gave me a thumbs-up and continued to snog his partner.

Once my legs reformed, I took Cynthia by the hand and hoisted myself up, heading for that alcove to reunite with Nanlee. I peeked inside to be certain it was him, and, *oh dear, I got an eyeful.* He and that girl I heard about were giving it to one another vigorously and *they seemed to fit well.*

I waited, ashamed to face him in such a circumstance, but I felt it was necessary.

'Hello, old chum,' I gulped.

Nanlee was still kissing.

I tapped him lightly upon the shoulder.

He grunted in response and looked up. 'Alec!'

There was a quick pause of a final kiss with his girl. Then, Nanlee stood up and gave me a hug. 'It has been a questionable experience.'

'You're telling me. Who's the girl?'

Nanlee held his hand out to her. 'This is Aphrothia, a friend of mine.'

'Obviously a very good friend to give you comfort like that,' I nattered.

I shook hands with Aphrothia and I introduced her to Cynthia.

'Of all things, I thought I was alone in the world,' she exclaimed.

Cynthia was taken aback by this, and upon looking closely, she saw a version not unlike herself.

'Hi, twin,' Cynthia giggled.

'It seems you must be my better half,' Aphrothia observed.

'Sad case, then,' I guessed.

Nanlee took over, stating confidently. 'It was, but I have sorted the young mess out and she will cry no more.'

Cynthia asked Nanlee, 'Are you serious with her?'

He sucked in a breath. 'No offence to you, my dear, but, yes I am. I took her from the hostile dregs of life and transformed her. I have now been transformed myself and there is no going back.'

I was now shocked. 'So, you plan to remain a Mercaste?'

'No, what I meant was... I found this female very special. Yes, a hard case, but special in my eyes. We worked it out together and realised we found delight in each other's company.'

'Friends, still, at least?'

Cynthia was so insecure.

'Always.' Nanlee gave her a hug. 'And your pairing with Alec seems to me the *correct* course of justice.'

I looked lovingly at Cynthia. 'We can be together. Nanlee has his girl. I now have mine.'

Cynthia jumped excitedly. 'By Jove, we've got it!'

Aphrothia saw her counterpart's glee and whinged. 'I do not know why *you* are so damn happy. You and your friend were written in the stars. It does not take a 'Stotle to figure that one out, duh!'

I did not know how to take this... backhander, but I just went with the flow of things. *The space of things could wait 'til later.* It was lucky I was used to the quirks of Mercastes, especially those who had a rough Mortal life. *Hers must have been a doozy!*

'I appreciate your sentiment, miss,' I told her, 'You should be as happy as my Cynthia. You've got a very rare specimen in Nanlee to see to your forever needs.'

As long as he doesn't get tinned-up by Raybin!

Nanlee and Aphrothia gazed at each other, 'We could be forever mates... even wed, if ye'd like,' he added.

Aphrothia went all pragmatic. 'Sounds like a logical step. I have no family and neither have you.'

'At least I have the better half,' I chuckled, glancing at Cynthia, kissing her.

'I must challenge ye on that one, Alec,' Nanlee argued. He rebelled against being combative and allowed himself to feel good for Aphrothia's sake. He kissed her, too.

I then decided to tell him about my meeting with Raybin.

Nanlee freaked out. 'You did WHAT?!'

'I have seen, confronted and put him to size,' I proudly confirmed.

'You faced that son of a so-and-so? After what he had done to me?!'

'And what he has done to Neptune's Own,' I added.

'I uncovered the dealings with the fisheries; hence why you found the invoice in my office,' Nanlee said. 'I was about to speak to Raybin about it when...'

'Yes,' I paused.

'He doesn't he realise what he did...'

I stood ground, my eyes fixed at him. 'His action of dumping you in the tank led you to meet Aphrothia.'

'Yes, there is that,' he admitted.

'It will have to be dealt with. It is one thing to show fish and cast them out freely, but selling to a factory for profit is another.'

'That's madness,' Nanlee agreed.

'That bill in your office was for a high amount.'

'I had not gotten to it, as I was thrown into the tank before I could take action. I was wondering if that was why I was mistaken for you, you know, as an excuse for a cover-up,' Nanlee pondered.

'Perhaps, but I wouldn't worry about it. When I made mention of his night time stunts, he got defensive about it. I bet you he was most likely drunk.'

'Too out of character though,' Nanlee sighed. 'It did not seem right.'

Nanlee and I looked at Cynthia and Aphrothia chatting away, like scroll-ends that belonged together. A likely pair, and if it were one's decision, *one would take both.*

Just like Nanlee and I...

... if such decision was made by a woman.

The four of us headed back into the sea to converse with Neptune, for there was much to discuss.

CHAPTER XVI

We raced within our watery realm to find my Lord, Neptune. The cascading waters with sparkly eyes cast a shadowy net over us, to which we found rather alluring. *He was truly a presence in and of Himself.*

''Tis I, do not be afraid, my children,' He announced.

Nanlee came to his senses. 'Ah, it's you. Might have known.'

I took hold of Cynthia's hand. 'It's now or never. I hope you have made a decision.'

'Indeed, I have,' she said.

'Good.' We looked at one another and kissed; she was cooing at me with doe eyes.

A thunderous roar had interrupted our small refrain.

'Cynthia Tarquinne, are you willing to commit to the sea?'

She trembled a bit, throwing in a curtsey to show respect. 'I am ready and willing to do as Your Lordship sees fit.'

'That is fabulous. But you must come closer to Me,' Neptune bellowed.

She approached the grand Lord with awe and concern. She didn't fear Him, and felt at ease within His light. Her concern regarded her not telling her companions, the Threescore, at what she was about to undergo. That would have to be dealt with later, as difficult as it will be to explain to them.

For the moment, she was under His command. He kissed her again and suddenly, her legs transformed into a slightly bulbous fin, owing to an annoyingly wide hip shape. Nanlee, Aphrothia and I witnessed the occurrence, with our fins swishing about wildly. We were pleased she became one of us... and there was no turning back, *unless by choice*. Most Mercastes, however, usually remain so, after their transformations, due to not wanting to *ever* return and resume a detestable life on land.

Cynthia was most shapely in my eyes and I felt myself the luckiest person alive.

'Well done, ol' girl.'

'I'm now one of you. It sure feels strange. I can understand your earlier difficulty.'

'No need for pity now. We have work to do,' I hesitated, gulping a bit of water, 'Shall we marry?'

'Are you proposing? Gosh, this is sudden.'

'Umm, you agreed to commit to the sea and, if further wanting, myself, if I am not mistaken.'

'I was told to commit to the sea,' she recalled.

I pressed more. 'Do you want to marry me, or Nanlee?'

She looked at Nanlee and felt it wrong to disrupt the relationship he was having with Aphrothia. If Aphrothia was a sad case as she displayed, then *Nanlee* should bear that burden. Cynthia thus decided to leave them free to do each other's bidding.

'I shall marry you, Alec. Nanlee seems more occupied and I think Aphrothia deserves such a man, as gentlemanly as he is,' Cynthia consented.

YIPPEEE!!!! The wait was over.

She went over to Nanlee and Aphrothia. 'You have my blessing if you two wish togetherness. Pray no offence that I did not choose you,' she gave Nanlee a kiss.

Nanlee understood... *fully*. 'My dear, we will always be friends and I firmly believe that is what we were in the first place. Love comes later, even if it is with someone else.'

Cynthia was astounded. 'You are most kind. You are not an average Mortal, are you?'

'I am no longer Mortal,' Nanlee blurted through the wet swirl. 'My life has changed, and my course is clearer.'

'I think I can say the same,' Cynthia agreed.

'My blessing goes with thee.' Nanlee turned to Aphrothia. 'Marriage, then?'

'I guess,' Aphrothia droned, 'I've no one anyway, so let's get it done.'

'You sound like you're about to undertake a school exam.'

'A school exam would be easier if one studied for it.'

Nanlee was now questioning her integrity. 'So you do not wish this? I must know now. If you come across as a depressive wife, what would others say? I *thought* you were getting better.'

'Stick it in their fish bones. I don't care either way,' came the snapback.

Neptune knew the quarrel was a front on her part. The dear lass had been treated so roughly and her mistrust knew no bounds, even toward those who shown kindness toward her, like Nanlee. 'Aphrothia, this fellow had supported you since finding you alone at the sea wreckage. Nanlee has been a perfect companion to you. You're not getting any younger and you've got a ready made Mercaste willing to love you past your flaws. Now, how about it, eh?'

'Can we? Shall we? Oh, please,' Nanlee pleaded.

Aphrothia looked around the shell-green world. True, she was not pining for anyone in particular. Her family were assholes at the best of times, and had revealed their nasty side toward her. *They would have made her marry a crappy toff anyway.*

She returned her gaze to Nanlee, who offered himself to her *freely.* 'Alright, let's do it.'

They hugged and Nanlee replied, 'I knew I could get past that crustacean-style shell of yours.'

Neptune cleared His throat and the bubbles quivered around us. 'Let us begin.'

He officiated the four-tailed, double marriage ceremony. The fabled words were spoken, vows made and adhered to, forever more. Neptune supplied special wedding rings for Cynthia and Aphrothia, whilst Nanlee and I received plain bands. The fish in the sea rejoiced all the same, and some of them were jumping out and into the water with glee. They made such a fuss that passer-by Mortals on the pier grumbled under their breath, with the little noise that was made.

Oddly coincidental, the Mortals who passed by were none other than the Threescore, who were out on an afternoon stroll... doing things men at *their* age like to do.

Cateliffe noticed the ripples and splashes. 'Those fish out there seem livelier than ever.'

Maybe they are awaiting the canning,' Nay-Smith thought.

'Nah,' Buckingham interjected, 'There is something fishy going on. Those guys out there look too happy to be worried about canning. I think we should stay and watch what happens.'

The three men remained at the pier for a quarter of an hour. The hoopla subsided and the gaiety was over.

'Let's go to the Plaza and eat. I'm hungry,' Nay-Smith suggested.

The others agreed and they went on their way...

... whilst undersea, Nanlee, myself and our wives spent time together, feasting alongside Neptune. There, I broke the news about Raybin and the goings-on at the Circus.

Neptune, being omnipotent, already knew of it. 'I have been aware of this Mortal for some time, watching his every move. He is a smile-rag, but I am giving him an opportunity to change his ways.'

'I only just discovered it when I was thrown in the tank,' Nanlee said. 'I would have put a stop to this, and I wonder if that was the real reason Raybin made that excuse that I looked like Alec when he had me dumped in.'

'The man does not see reason,' I explained, 'He lives in a bottom of a glass of his own making and floats atop at times. I found him very evasive, but I was persistent.'

'Oh, really?' Neptune rolled his eyes in a sarcastic fashion.

Nanlee turned to me, 'How could he mistake you for me?'

'How else could he be that daft in putting wool over people's eyes? They pay to see live fish, and expect them to carry on living. They do not know whence they go afterwards,' I retorted, 'Or care, for that matter.'

'But *I do*, in both cases,' Neptune replied.

'I heard my companions make fish jokes on a recent visit to them when I introduced Alec,' Cynthia pouted.

'I do recall,' I remarked, 'And I did not care for that Mortal humour of theirs, either.'

'Nor I,' Nanlee added, 'Now that I am a fish, I feel complete. As a researcher, I can now see the whole picture, and it has been a most fascinating journey.'

Aphrothia put in her say. 'I guess it is alright, when you want to live elsewhere or are *forced to*.'

What a way with words. *Good luck, Nanlee!*

'You depressing little shit,' Cynthia rebuked her, 'I let Nanlee go, so that you can have someone, as I had found Alec. How could you disrespect such a beautiful person? He's a good man. Please treat him as such.'

'I confess that it has been most fruitful with him,' she admitted.

Neptune smiled at Aphrothia. 'I know you've been put through a ringer not of your choosing. I want to make it up to you.' A wave of His lent into her space and a breath of fresh air, erm... water, had enclosed her. Inside, she felt a soft healing sensation, somewhat... she was unsure. *I guess if one got close to a god, one would heal nicely...*

... but for Aphrothia, it could take a circular staircase of many steps to get her there.

The Water Lord then gave us marching orders. 'I want you to go forth, away from an old guy like Me. Enjoy yourselves, procreate, you know... *have fun.* I've heard Clunia's a good shag-spot and if you wish to visit or live in the Mortal's world, you may. But, you will not have long to do so.'

My eyes widened. 'Why? What are you planning?'

His tone was evasive. 'Oh, my dear child, nothing for you to be concerned about. Just a small token of Myself I do not want the Mortals to forget. I shall not trouble you with the details, for it is a god's work. You're a Mercaste and not sophisticated enough to understand.'

My emotions peaked further in curiosity.

The god smiled at us and myself, specifically. 'If you do return to the Mortal's world, I will give you good fare and time for yourselves. When the time comes, you will all be ordered to return to sea. I can make manifest anywhere, even in a glass of water (if you do not drink it, of course).

We smiled at His little joke.

'We shall obey thee,' Nanlee bowed down.

'You can count on us,' I shouted, as the watery eclipse swirled around us. We were then waved along until we reached the familiar sand beach of Clunia.

Cynthia used her new fin with delight. 'Wow, this is truly something. Now, how do I get out of here?'

The rest of us laughed. I crawled toward her. 'You roll unto the land. The Mercastes will give you cloth to dry yourself off, so you may be less challenged.'

The Mercastes ashore had seen us, waved, and, just as I said, had much cloth to dry us off with. One of them headed directly for Cynthia.

It was Colpert.

'Congratulations on your new acquisition,' he said, indicating her fin and giving her a cloth.

'Thank you,' Cynthia replied, using it to dry off with.

Colpert stared at me, 'Hello again, Alec. I see you've taken the swim with her.'

'We indeed took the plunge together,' I noted.

Everyone laughed. Then Nanlee stated, 'Neptune's planning something. We do not have much time. I need to get to my flat and spend time with Aphrothia.'

Colpert was surprised when he saw the wedding band. 'You too, Nan? You all got hitched?'

'We did, respectively,' I clarified. 'Neptune performed a double wedding for us.'

'That's rich. Now, you are all married to one another,' Colpert smirked.

'I'm Cynthia's and Aphrothia belongs to Nanlee,' I stated.

'It looks like you are all dry. You will need tunics if you remain landed on Mortal soil. I'll get you some,' Colpert offered, and walked away.

'Cheers,' Nanlee said. He looked at Aphrothia, and, as a good husband should, gave her a sweet kiss on the lips. They stayed that way for some time.

'Shall we?' Cynthia also gave me a kiss, and we filled our souls.

Colpert returned with tunics for all of us, which we put on.

'If you're staying on, there's a chariot race tomorrow in the morning. It's Ben-Phurr against Viamaturio. Should be fun.'

Cynthia squealed, 'That would be most exciting, wouldn't it?'

'I will give it consideration,' I winked at her. 'You just like looking at the racers, don't you?'

'I'd be lying to you if there was nothing for me to look at,' Cynthia confessed.

I tousled her hair a bit and grinned. 'Women!'

'Let's go to the flat first to get our bearings. It had been awhile, remember,' Nanlee recommended.

'I think it would be prudent to visit the Threescore; maybe tell them about Neptune's plan, as well,' Cynthia suggested.

I rocked my head to the side. 'Why should we tell those silly-old-farts about that?'

'Usually when a god has a plan, I reckon it to be a coming disaster. Gods are known to get temperamental, and with Neptune and his temper... *all* will go mental,' Nanlee warned.

'I never took you for a religious sort,' I said to him.

'You never asked and I never discuss. Religion is personal and is just as intimate as going to one's toilet,' he remarked, recalling Aphrothia's earlier comment.

Colpert looked at Aphrothia. 'Pretty good catch you got, Nanlee. I'm going now. Maybe I will see you at the races.'

'Bye for now,' I called.

He walked away and the four of us took a ferry to Pallancium. Some old coins put in the tunic pockets by Mercastes, saw to our passage. We headed for Nanlee's place and that evening, we planned to pay a visit to the Threescore.

CHAPTER XVII

We spent the rest of the day at Nanlee's flat, where I finally released myself from that dreaded beard! I happily shaved it off with excited relief, mostly anticipating Cynthia's reaction. *She'd squeal, I could feel it!* The four of us, respectively, coupled up and made a tidy outlay of love, Clunian-style, separately and communally. Behind closed doors, an orgy could be found anywhere...

... and here was no exception...

... and Mercastes were great admirers of this.

As I made love to Cynthia, a poem struck me, as I wallowed in pure thought and ecstasy.

I want to wow you in my own bed,
And tickle the hairs beneath your lagoon.
If not for the curly fairness,
I'd a-ridden thee!
Love lifts tonight,
As the whole of my being
Swam forth
Into the depths of your person.
You cast an eye upon the shadow
Of my body.
Cornering every inch of my desire,
Oh, what a lovely maidstrom, indeed!

* * * * * *

I looked up from the sofa, I saw the calm view around me, which I found enchanting. As we had then separated and Nanlee went to his room with Aphrothia, I heard sparse noises coming from behind the closed door. It doesn't take one far to figure out what *those two* were up to; I was not interested in seeing them grunt in completion.

Yet, I cared not a Cicero in the slightest, for my world was now secure in the person of Cynthia.

Later on, once we all had our fill, we each took turns in the bath. I found it invigorating, but I still yearned to be with Cynthia alone. *Ah well.* I defied the air by giving her small kisses on her neckline. Nanlee saw this and approached his dear lady in similar fashion. The four of us plunged into another Clunian love-making session before the sands of time in the hourglass revealed the intention of visiting Cynthia's companions later that evening.

We released ourselves hastily to prepare for the meeting and we left the flat to await the storm coming. I felt kind regards for Buckingham, Cateliffe and Nay-Smith, but I was certain they would be shocked at our newfound attachment.

I darkened the doorstep to find, after knocking, Cateliffe standing in the open passage. He caught Cynthia and my two other friends behind me.

'Ah, hello there, Cynthia. By quick shrift, you've returned. You're just in time for supper. Will you please come in?'

He held the door open to let us in. Buckingham and Nay-Smith sat lounging away on the sofa, reading scrolls and being old-folk.

Buckingham lifted his eyes away from his distraction to notice. 'What an interesting group we have here.'

Nanlee smiled, nervously. 'It's been some time, yes.'

'It has,' chimed Nay-Smith, fiddling with his spectacles and not taking his eyes off his scroll.

Buckingham put his attention toward Cynthia. 'You're looking well, tonight. What have you been up to?'

There was a feeling of slight embarrassment on her part at the hasty union we made together. Yet, she was brave enough to show off her new band.

'My, my,' Buckingham yelped at the sight of such a jewel. 'That must have been a pretty packet. I did not know an actor of the stage or a Mercaste would have that kind of funding.'

'It was given to me by Neptune Himself,' Cynthia revealed.

'Underwater treasures you Mortals miss out is our gain,' I said.

'Underwater mishaps are the least of our concerns,' Cateliffe dismissed, 'Still, I must congratulate you, nevertheless. Shall we to the table?'

We gathered at the table to see a lovely spread filled with bread, fish, meat, fruits of a varied sort and plenty of wine. These fellows really enjoyed living; one can see it in their waistline.

But, it was kind of them to share this with us.

Once we began to eat, Nay-Smith added with dogged eyes, 'It would have been nice to have been there.'

'It was a decision the four of us came to and agreed upon. The ceremony was held underwater and witnessed by many a colony of fish,' Nanlee said.

Cateliffe was surprised and freaked out. 'You can breath underwater, Cynthia?'

'Now I can and I have my tail, too,' she stated proudly.

'She looks a treat with it, oooh,' I smiled, taking a bite of bread.

Cateliffe recalled the lively celebration of fish above the sea at the time of our marriage. 'We passed by the noisy sea... that was you lot?'

'Aye, that it was,' I beamed.

Buckingham asked, 'So you are all married to one another?'

'Cynthia and I, Nanlee and Aphrothia, respectively,' I confirmed.

Aphrothia waved hello to the dear fellows, half-heartedly, then returned to finish her meal.

Nay-Smith was concerned. 'What's up with her?'

'A difficult life and a hard case, which I had corrected,' Nanlee informed him. He went on to tell about how they met and that he reached out to help her.

Cateliffe made an attempt to understand us. 'So you Mercastes are either criminals or hard luck cases?'

'Depends,' Nanlee replied, 'I became a Mercaste by accident when my superior, Raybin, had me thrown into the tank, thinking I was Alec. It was either I survive in the tank and become a Mercaste, or I die.'

I clarified the point. 'Neptune gives each person who enters His realm a Kiss, and the neck-gills form.' I showed them the mark. 'Then one gets the tailfin.'

The three men were enthralled at our story.

Nay-Smith seemed unsure. 'So you are not really fish, and not fully human, are you?'

'We are part of two worlds,' I explained, 'We can live and walk amongst Mortals and live and swim in the seas amongst the fish.'

Nay-Smith blushed heavily, dejected by all the mockery he had made in the past about fish.

However, Cateliffe still pushed the scroll around. 'Do you get reeled in by fisher-folk?'

I rolled my eyes at his jest, but took it lightly. 'We swim too deep for that. We tend to reside in caves or old, decrepit sunken barges. We sometimes mix with other fish, but just for a swim, not socially.'

Buckingham turned to Cynthia. 'So which world do you prefer most?'

She answered, 'The watery world is secluded, yet fascinating. Everyone gets on with living, or surviving, in some cases, but it is *not* an unworthy existence. There is an island we also reside on, if even for a rest, called Clunia. That is a comforting place, as one could stretch one's legs out, once dried.'

'Neptune is so inviting, and is all around you in the water,' Aphrothia added.

Nay-Smith's eyes widened. 'So you are familiar with a god?'

'Well, we all are. If we enter His realm, He looks after us,' Nanlee said, 'It is no big deal.'

'I'd say it is,' Buckingham bellowed, 'There are many gods about, but I have never seen any Mortal interaction with any of them.'

'You obviously haven't met Neptune,' Cynthia giggled.

We carried on eating and finishing off the wine. We remained together chatting into the night and later, took our leave back to Nanlee's, where we dropped down into the night, and more.

The next morning, as planned, we attended the chariot races at the *Pallandrome*. A huge turnout was evident all around us, the great majority of which were fans of the great Ben-Phurr; Viamaturio had his own admirers sprinkled within the audience. Compared to the races in Rome, (which were much more elaborate, with pomp, power, and human competition all played out, for better or worse), the races in Pallancium were quite mild, on a smaller scale, yet attracting as much enthusiasm as their Roman counterparts.

We paid the couple of denarii and sat at the rear of the complex, though we would have preferred a closer row. Those who waited from sunrise got the best of views; some of them even encamped outside the area, overnight! Still, it was acceptable nonetheless and a fine place to sneak in a kiss or two; very similar to the overcrowded theatre of my day.

We sat together, waiting for the start. Colpert turned up and joined us.

'I see you made it alright,' he said.

'Wouldn't miss it for all the water in the world,' I replied.

'Spoken like a true Mercaste,' Colpert laughed, 'There are others here too, all dispersed. So, how's married life?'

'Fine,' I answered, holding Cynthia's hand.

Colpert gave Cynthia some attention. 'And how are you doing, young lady?'

She giggled shyly and nuzzled against me.

'I take that as a yes,' he quipped.

Nanlee offered to buy refreshments, as a drink wouldn't go amiss...

... and when he returned, the drinks were most welcome and refreshing on a hot day.

However, my drink came to life. A voice emerged from the depths of my cup.

'Alec...'

My mind raced before the event started. 'Cynthia, was that you?'

'Nope,' she gulped down her drink already.

'Nanlee?'

His mouth was occupied too, *with his wife...*

I sighed and looked down.

The voice returned. 'It is I, Neptune.'

'Ah, the cup of wine trick. Very funny.'

'Tis no laughing matter, son.'

Colpert stared at me. 'Did you say something?'

I blushed. 'Ermm... no. I...'

'Never mind.'

I waited for the god to continue. *Lucky, I did not have to wait long.*

'I know where you are,' He said, 'And I want to keep My children safe. You're attending the races, are you not?'

'Yes, sir,' I replied.

'There is no time for chatter. Listen and do not question. When the race is finished, you and yours must leave Pallancium, if you want to survive. All of you must go. Pass the message amongst our kind.'

The voice faded.

And I got worried.

Really worried.

I whispered to Colpert, 'We must return to the sea after the event. Neptune's orders. Pass it on.'

'Right-o,' he got up and spread the news.

I also informed Cynthia, Nanlee and Aphrothia.

'Awh, I was hoping we could remain just a tad longer,' Aphrothia whinged.

'If you want to live, ol' girl, you shall do as your god saith,' Nanlee insisted. 'Once this is finished, we head to the water.'

Cynthia asked, 'I wonder what He's planning?'

'Whatever it is, it will be big and I do not wish to get caught up in a rage, especially a rage of a god. Too much, man; that is too much,' I moaned. 'He certainly would not use a throwaway wine goblet to warn me if it wasn't important enough.'

Suddenly, a loud klaxon had sounded, heralding in the start of the race. The two opponents entered the track area, with horses in fancy plumage and coverings marking respective insignias. The men looked fancy themselves, in their respective gear and handsome faces. The crowd squealed and shrieked over their hero, Ben-Phurr, whilst some others from outer parts of the town had rooted for Viamaturio (though his earful was less intense). They were not fresh-on-the-scene bucks, but mature competitors in their late thirties, constantly at it for years, performing 'round the Empire for the masses.

A small ceremonial parade was held where the two men rode out together for the crowd to have a good swoon over them. *This helped develop morale and good cheer.* Sometimes, there had been foul play between other racers on previous occasions; the races themselves usually fared well and gave displaced Romans and native Britons something to watch and be entertained by. The competitions cemented the glory of Rome and were made memorable for many.

Ben-Phurr and Viamaturio took their places and drove their horses around the track six times until the winner was declared. The race went too fast, in my opinion, and it was over just as soon as it started. Other races would take place later, but this one was the more favoured, as *these* competitors were the best in the Empire.

After the short spell, Viamaturio claimed the victory this time. Ben-Phurr, the more popular one, took it well, shaking his opponent's hand.

'We should wrestle next time to decide truly who is best,' Ben-Phurr suggested.

'It will make a goodly change to racing. I've always wanted to tackle you down,' Viamaturio replied.

'I think the maiden-folk will love that,' Ben-Phurr smirked.

'You wish,' came the stiff answer.

The two men laughed themselves into their changing rooms. Young girls had waited for them, wanting a piece of *them*, and not just for signatures. They lusted greedily over them both. The hot bathing facilities provided a sumptuous haven for them. We, however, did not stay long and returned to the sea, as Neptune ordered. Other Mercastes, including Colpert, dived in as well, swimming deep and away from Pallancium.

CHAPTER XVIII

The fate of Pallancium hung in the balance. At this point, Neptune had enough of His share of horrid Mortals and wished death upon them *all*. He cemented His wishes into action and the surrounding waters rose to a great height. A surge had formed and encroached on Pallancium's harbour. Waves began to rock violently and water raced throughout the winding streets, not unlike a chariot race... *but with no competition*. It was Neptune and all Neptune... almighty, fierce, and proud... and He did not like getting angry...

... the problem was, this time... He was.

He let loose on the Mortal's world faster than lightning, and even Jupiter had to take a back seat for a change. Neptune's waves ran rings around Saturn's work in the fields, dampening them in the process. Buildings were pounded upon until the facades caved in. That Aquarium, which focused on His children in particular, had the most damage set upon it, due to Raybin's attitude and actions against them.

The sea took shape in its most rigid form and rose further upon the land mass. The Mercastes on Clunia took cover in the sea, as Neptune struck at anything that was not water-based. They knew no one, nor the land itself, could survive His temper tantrums. Water swelled in all directions, flooding gardens and concrete centres alike. Those in public places were the first victims of this deluge. Other people in homes, or shoppes, remained inside, though doubtful they would remain alive. Rain and rushing sea flowed rapidly through every crack and crevice of concrete. Casualties piled higher than a mountain range and there seemed to be no end in sight.

Some Mortals tried to flee the disaster, heading for the inner regions of Britannia. One place considered was the nearby Whitfir Valley, where a clot of citizens congregated.

It was far enough away from the sea and many who decided to settle there, saw it fit to make the area home. They rebuilt their lives and reckoned they'd be safe from Neptune's water-ride.

The whole sea felt alive and it was a funny sensation to swim around in. I took Cynthia deep into the realm and sought that shipwreck I found so comforting. We rode Neptune's storm from within and held one another tightly. I had no idea what happened to Nanlee and Aphrothia... I thought they had followed us, yet, I gathered they had their own destiny to go towards. I figured they would seek out a cave to be alone; *one's guess is as good as another.* I did hope once this passed, that we would meet again.

Cynthia and I remained below and lived within the shipwreck. We made ourselves a small nest and enjoyed the Mortal's once lavish environment. The coverage inside bore the finest delights humanly possible at the time... even I had not experienced such splendour in my day as an actor. However, Fate had not separated it from the moments to come. I was unsure how badly Neptune would strike ashore and I wondered about Cynthia's mid-aged companions. I did hope they sought themselves somewhere to go... for there was no warning them... *I only just found out.* And I could not speak of it, unless I knew what it was to speak of. There should be fertile places about, *other* than Pallancium.

Word came to me that even the beloved Amphitheatre had been levelled into a watery grave. I could not contain myself and cried bitterly over it... but the water around me had hid my tears well. I cried for the family that rejected me and the many colleagues with whom I worked for much of my career. I suddenly experienced a lucid moment through sour tears, when I thought about my ex-wife and the children. Would *they* be clever enough to escape Neptune's wrath?

I heavily reflected and I caught Cynthia swimming over to me, ready for a keen embrace. Her tail surrounded me with love and it was difficult to push away from her deepest affection.

'The people we once knew are probably dead by now; we cannot sink ourselves down like this,' she said.

I gazed at her and in my grief, I called unto Neptune and prayed for an answer to my inner torment.

As the Mortal bashing continued, a voice boomed at me. 'What is it now, Alec? Can't you see I'm busy? It's the end of the world, you know.'

'My Lord and my god... what happened to my family?'

'Why do you want to know? They ditched you, remember, and so did your own society. *Who gives a fuck about them,*' came the resentful answer.

'Please... I need to know... I'll...,' I begged.

'Awh, hush up, child and come here.' Neptune reached out to me and sat me on His knee. 'You care very much for them, despite them sending you down to My care.'

I sniffed, snivelled and secreted tears more saltier than a container of sea-salt.

The god looked at me in a rare, passive moment. 'They are fine. In fact, all your friends, companions, and everyone who loved and knew you are alright. My apocalypse did not include *everybody*, you know.'

'So the ol' lady is alright?'

'Yea and somewhere else, possibly with *someone else*... I think in the Mediterranean part of My realm.'

'And the children?'

'Older, with her, and most likely birthing their own by now... *sorry.*'

'Nought to worry, sir.' I sighed with relief. Now, I can move on in life... *nought to past thoughts... ever!*

...but...

'What about Nanlee, Aphrothia, and Cynthia's old-man companions?'

'Escaped. Nanlee took Aphrothia toward the deeper waters of the Continent, maybe Rome, for all I know. *Why would a god care?* Those three men... they saw what was happening and after a good splash on their doorstep (of which I am quite proud), they fled inland. Last I heard... *lest I care.*'

'These are Your children,' I argued.

'Yes, Nanlee and Aphrothia are My children. The rest are not and you better mind yourself towards Me, sir!'

Snidey-face!

The god read my mind. 'You find it novel speaking to me, don't you, acting as if I were a fellow Mortal.'

I gulped, realising I crossed a line. 'Umm... no... I.'

Neptune had felt tossed about by me for long enough. His next bellow echoed a tirade of complexion I shall never forget.

'Mortal scum! I would truly advise you to live elsewhere, for you shall no longer be part of My realm. I recommend the Whitfir Valley; it sounds hospitable for you. You may keep your special indulgences I gave you for the time being, until *My* will has been completed. When you feel the calm in the water, you and yours must flee. I love you both deeply and now that Pallancium has had its day, you will no longer need to remain under-the-sea. There is no charge against you, for you committed no crime. Divorce is not illegal, is it? You do not belong here, long term.'

'So I may return to Mortal flesh?'

'On a permanent basis, yes.'

Wow, I can become fully human again, and breathe in the air, as nature had intended me to do.

The god took His leave and left me with Cynthia. The violence in the water continued another week or so, never letting up. We hid inside the shipwreck and lived there for the duration. It was nice to sleep above water, though for some reason, it was just as comfortable beneath. I cuddled and huddled with Cynthia for much of the time, feeding on small fish. Day by day, it felt like eternity, to dwell here for so long, counting on the time until we must leave here forever.

One day, I swam to take a peek above level to see the results of Neptune's rave. There was not much left of Pallancium. Water damage permeated everywhere and it looked permanently deserted. Nor was Clunia to be found... it had been submerged and broken up, sunken to the bottom of the sea. As I thought, the Aquarium was hit the hardest, due to Raybin's most pugnacious personality. It was *unlikely* he survived this at all...

I returned under and found my dear wife holding a metal object in her hand. She showed it to me and it was that bent sword I'd found some time back. I'd say it was the luckiest charm ever, created by a Mortal.

I spoke, 'We shall keep this as a parting present from Neptune, eh?'

'Parting?'

Oops, I forgot to tell Cynthia...

'We need to leave here soon and make ready for the Whitfir Valley. We can forge a new life together, you and I,' I smiled.

She looked at me. 'This is a just a bent sword; a forge could fix it... wait, what do you mean we have to leave here?'

'No time to share. We have to go. I shall discuss it with you upon land.' She gave me the sword. 'I think this could make a fab trinket, a bit clanky, though.'

I took the sword and found some stringy substance to secure it to me.

'Hey, watch it,' the ball shape surrounding the string yelled.

'Oh, dear. So sorry. I did not know you were there.'

'Bloody Mortals, ye are,' the entity muttered to itself, half asleep.

When I realised it was an octopus, I swam away quickly before it nailed me with ink.

I then had a run-in with the crab, which I saved from being eaten, when Cynthia and I previously visited Clunia.

'Top o'the tail to ye,' it said, with the throng of its family following into the distance.

Meanwhile, Cynthia found some old rope from the ship and we used that instead...

... and at least, it didn't talk back!

We later swam away from Pallancium's shores to find the Whitfir Valley.

CHAPTER XIX

The Whitfir Valley was a good distance away, and the Mortal survivors of the flooding were hearty enough to make the journey. Of course, they would go on foot, but if one was lucky, one could ride a horse. The neighbouring Centaurs gave lifts to those more weary. The Centaurs came in handy as imports from the Greek islands, and a passage on them made for very lively conversation. *One could never bore with a Centaur.* They were intelligent creatures and knew how to get about. They were preferred over horses for long range journeys, whilst horses made perfect work animals and short-hop transport... *at least they could not complain openly!*

On the other hand, the Mercastes did not care one way or another to seek new land, because they could just swim for it. The flooding did not devastate our community, though Clunia was destroyed in the widespread tempest. The Mercastes that longed for land, swam to other shores in the area and a few of them just remained underwater... to live out their days as fish, forever forgetting about their *human* past.

As Neptune commanded us, Cynthia and I swam towards the Valley, along with some Mercastes who wished to return to the land. The advantage we had was that we did not need to go on foot, and used our fins to seek out our new life together. Though we were unfamiliar with the area outside Pallancium, there were Mercastes helpful enough to give us directions. It was brand new territory to explore, either by sea or land, but the air would give the greatest advantage. Unfortunately, Mortals and Mercastes did not boast wings. The Sirens had them, but they were not the most sociable folk, nor friendly enough to give counsel. They were in it for themselves, just singing along and causing trouble for most.

It took some time for us to get there and we took it slowly. The sea was livelier then usual, due to the tempest. *Disorientation filled the waves...*

We spent as much time in the water as possible, before we had to renounce our piscine existence. We bade farewell to the Mercastes who saw us leave.

One of them approached us. 'You are still welcome here. Neptune had not fully rejected you, Alec. His temper got the better of Him and it consumed His judgement.'

'Thank you,' I smiled back, 'Yet, I believe it is time for me and the wife to move on... to landed shores for the rest of our days.'

'We shall miss you; at least you've got someone to move on with,' came the fleeting response, before a tail emerged, bobbing up and down, aiming for the distance.

I sighed, saddened by the finality of it all and continued on nearer and nearer to our journey's end. I stuck my head above water to see where I was. *Now, I felt like a lost fish at sea.*

I saw someone on the shore, mending a net of some kind. He looked old and kindly, but I was timid to enquire as to where I was...

... so, bravery had to step forth...

I called out, 'I say, what is this place?'

The kindly gentleman looked up. 'Nice day for a swim, eh?'

'Where am I?'

'You're in the water,' he replied.

I tsked and tried once more. 'What place is this?'

'Ah, sorry. I could not hear you properly.' He came forward to me. 'You are in the Whitfir Valley area. The valley itself is further inland. I like the fishing out here.'

FISHING?

Cateliffe's earlier joke caught up with me. 'Umm... thank you.'

I swam away. We were here, but this fellow seemed a bit *off*, to me. He looked friendly enough, but I hoped he would not put *me* on the menu...

... so I went back to find Cynthia. We both took the risk and rolled out onto the shore.

The old man laughed. 'Oh my, two catches of the day.'

'Very funny. Do you have anything for us to dry off with?'

'I think I may have something. I bring linen with me to dry my catches too; I hope this is enough,' he paused, 'I say, you are Mercastes, aren't you? I thought they were just a silly myth.'

'Just like Centaur Transport? No way, we're no myth,' I laughed.

'Wow. What's it like being caught between two worlds?'

This fellow was inquisitive.

I gave a thought. 'Ummm, interesting, especially when one is completely dry and the legs reform.'

'You have legs?'

'Uh, yes. We wouldn't be Mercastes if we didn't,' Cynthia replied.

'Right,' the old man paused, then introduced himself. 'By the way, my name is Wolverton Harris.'

'Glad to meet you. I am Alexander Nespor, and this is my wife, Cynthia.'

'Charmed lady, I'm sure.' He stooped down to kiss her hand. 'Where were you coming from? I doubt that you took a mere stroll.'

'We did not. We came from Pallancium, living in the sea and on the island of Clunia.'

'Pallancium,' Harris muttered. 'They have those weird legalities where myth and reality converge.'

'Yes. I was cast out of town. Cynthia chose to join me.'

'Ah... well, you may join us. I want to form a community and we need new members.'

'I see,' I said, noticing my legs had emerged. I checked Cynthia and she was also humanised. I gave her the linen to cover herself up with.

Harris noticed me... *altogether*. 'I'll have to scrape around for something for you. Just a tick.'

He walked away and Cynthia and I huddled together to hide my bareness, when three familiar people stood before us.

'Cynthia?'

She looked up. 'Cateliffe!' She got up and gave him a hug; the linen, meanwhile, fell loosely around her.

'Oh Jupe,' she cried, grabbing the cloth for modesty.

Buckingham admired the view, but kept his politeness. Nay-Smith ogled a bit, yet spoke no *come-hithers*, either.

'It is good to see you all,' Cynthia said, composing herself well. 'How did you get here?'

'Centaur Transport, of course. We weren't going to walk, just cos a crazy-bum of a god wished to flush us out,' Nay-Smith replied.

'It certainly was a most lively experience. We barely had time to escape when we got hit at our doorstep,' Buckingham explained.

'Neptune told me about that,' I grinned. 'He said He was most proud of that.'

'I bet he was,' Cateliffe dismissed. 'Where's Nanlee and that girl we met?'

'I was told he was safe and heading elsewhere, to different shores and different lands, maybe,' I thought aloud.

'I don't know how many of us survived, but it is good to see you, Alec and Cynthia.' Buckingham gave us a hug.

'It was a bad day for Him and He took all of us with it,' I surmised.

At that point, Wolverton Harris returned with spare clothing for Cynthia and myself, (most nice of him), and greeted the Threescore.

'I only caught a bit of what you said; I did not mean to overhear, but it sounded like something big happened,' he said.

'Neptune went ape on us and flushed Pallancium like a *latrinum*,' I stated, putting on the native garment.

Wolverton was concerned for us. 'Gosh. It looks like you've had a nasty shock.'

He then introduced himself to the Threescore, and offered us something to eat. Later on, we were invited to meet other members of his group. There were quite a few, but the ones I felt most close to were Wilset, Tudmond, Greyrivers, Clivetum and Clarence. It seemed we would become a most jolly group in the Valley.

There were other tribal groups about, scattered throughout Roman Britain. Some of them chose Roman ways and became part of Imperial society. Others, like what Wolverton's group were becoming, wanted to remain as native Britons, and live as such. Some time ago, a tribe had gone against Roman rule, which I thought was rather daring, if not needless. The concept of tribes coming up against Imperial forces had sent a shiver down many a back of natives. The tribe who dared, led by a fiery warrior Queen called Boudicca, had taken matters into their own hands and fought bitterly against the Rule.

When they were put down by Roman soldiers, Boudicca was killed, or killed herself (one never knew from gossip), and most Britons remained quiet. Even a nearby tribe called the Isseums, had toned down their vivaciousness in clothing, attitude and tattoo art. They left their fabled village of I-Summora, near Londinium and headed elsewhere… *never to be seen again.*

Of course, someone down the time-line, with a bucket and spade, may find such a village, if they look hard enough…

We officially formed the Clubrit tribe, but a spelling error renamed the group the Clubretts. I liked the sound of it, as I had contributed the 'Clu' section, in tribute to Clunia. 'Brett' was originally Brit, for Britannia, but mistakes were made from which Mortals could never escape. So the name Clubrett was finalised and I was most pleased to be part of something more solid, compared to being part of something consisting of fragments of the many unhappy stories that composed the Mercastes. I remained close to the initial core of friends I just met. Women were plentiful, too and it did not take long to see our tribe grow in time.

I was asked if I had any skill or profession, to which I admitted being an actor.

'An actor's alright, but we have no need for amusements. We must have proper work for our community to build upon,' Buckingham argued.

'A land away from Rome, with us retaining our native tribal customs,' Wolverton added, 'These are caveman times.'

'I would hardly call the Roman Empire, caveman times,' Cateliffe piped up.

I breathed in a deep sigh, knowing I not only had to let go of the Mercaste existence, but to know that my acting skills were *not* required; well, *that was a heartbreak to say the least.*

I was put to work around the wooded areas and Cynthia and I made our settlement there. I became a woodsman and acquired carpentry skills to help build the community I now lived with. For the moment, I was happy to move on and be part of a group that was gregarious and unhampered by circumstance... *or the law.*

After a fashion, I decided to reinvent myself and change my name to Alexander Nespor Woodes. As being a woodsman was now my trade, I thought the new surname would make it easier to remember me by. Cynthia agreed to the change and was pleased for me.

She was also expecting a child, which made things more special, and I prepared myself for the occasion.

There were times when I looked back and thought about my life as an actor and a Mercaste; then Nanlee came to mind. I missed him terribly and made enquiries as to what happened to him. Word got back to me that he had made it to Rome and had a daughter who married into the powerful military family of Carmikulus. It was nice to know that he and Aphrothia made a success of themselves and enjoyed their married life together.

I also thought about Neptune and how He was getting on. Indeed, I could go to the well, pour myself a cup of water and speak into it, but *that* would make things awkward. *I would not do it.* Yet, a newfound respect for the sea and its creatures had been embedded in my mind, forever. Despite the perplexity, I wondered if I *should* share my story about my experiences as a Mercaste to the others...

... um, maybe later...

www.ingramcontent.com/pod-product-compliance
Lightning Source LLC
Chambersburg PA
CBHW020614120726
47905CB00003B/795